I'LL
NEVER
LEAVE
YOU

I'LL NEVER LEAVE YOU

Lennox Rex

I'LL NEVER LEAVE YOU

a collection of short stories

LENNOX REX

THE LAUGHING MAN HOUSE PUBLISHING

I'LL NEVER LEAVE YOU

Copyright © 2024 by The Laughing Man House and Lennox Rex

ISBN: 979-8-9996247-0-3

www.lmhpub.com

Cover Design by Mitch Green

Edited by Anna Corbeaux

Author photo by Holly Sivils

Royalty-Free images sourced by Pixabay

To Diane Ainsworth
I'm eternally grateful for your presence in my life, from my first day in your third-grade classroom to now.

To Beth
For all the books we devoured side by side in blanket forts, and the time we very nearly became blood siblings.

Table of Contents

Asterix [*] denotes content warning at the back of the book.

KNOW THYSELF

I never have trusted mirrors.

Or, to put a finer point on it, maybe it's always been that doppelgänger on the other side of the glass that puts my brain on high alert. The longer I stare into my own eyes without blinking, the less and less sense my face makes and the louder my mind insists, *This is not you.*

Something about watching my reflected lips twitch and twist into such uncanny smiles and seeing my own eyes narrow and glint with a hint of malice has always raised the tiny hairs on the back of my neck. Sometimes, watching those fleeting expressions feels like an act of defiance. "Prove it," I find myself whispering, "prove you're me." Most of the time I pull away, slightly shaken, and silently reassure myself, *That wasn't you, it's not you.*

Today, I choose to smile at that man in the glass and watch him mimic me as I adjust my tie in Mom's full-length mirror.

It's a family heirloom, the looking glass, crafted a handful of generations ago by some male relative that made fine furnishings. The dark cherry stain on cherrywood, with its inlaid gold, makes it almost regal. The four feet are carved to resemble the gnarled roots of a tree growing up into two separate trunks, the mirror's hinges serving as the tree's crown. The top of the frame holds a wonderful skyscape of wispy clouds that has always seemed so real as to be drifting lazily at the behest of the breeze. The same soft breath of air stirs up the golden leaves scattered along the bottom of the mirror's frame. I've always marveled at this looking glass for its obvious beauty, but that's not to say I ever trusted it. After all, we know how I feel about mirrors.

Mom appears in the glass, tilting her face up slightly as her thin lips curve into an adoring smile. "Of course I'd find you here."

I watch her movements in the glass as she reaches up to pat my arm.

"No need to preen," she teases. "You always look like my perfect gentleman."

I turn away from our reflections and bend down to plant a fleeting kiss on her forehead. "Finally dropping the 'little,' are we?" I tease right back.

She pauses to check her own appearance, giving herself an exaggerated smile and quickly rubbing a spot of lipstick off one of her front teeth. "Well, I suppose it had to happen someday." She punctuates her statement with a theatrical sigh before beaming up at me. "Thank you for making the time to visit. It means so much to your sister."

I choose not to remark on that. I think we both know perfectly well that Mom wanted me here more than Laura ever would. Though, I suppose, when you've moved back home to be with family while your husband deploys for who knows how long, you stop being so picky about the company you keep. The quickness with which she pulled me into a tight hug upon my arrival yesterday certainly took me by surprise. "Of course." I glance back to our reflections. "I'll be right down, okay?"

I give her one last peck on the forehead, and she chuckles on her way out of the room. "I'm not sure if it's that mirror you love or your own reflection."

An honest frown flits across my face as I give myself one last appraisal. To say I'm not looking forward to this farewell party is an understatement. Some would claim I'm a touch antisocial. Truth be told, I'm not exactly thrilled to be back home at good old 107 Fern Street, either. I suppose I might be able to get out of my usual yearly visit, since I've come now. So, there is some silver lining to this cloud. "Here goes nothing," I sigh. At least I don't have to carpool with Laura. Between her puffy-eyed sniffling and my niece's hysterics, I'd probably—

My muscles tense and my eye twitches at the ungodly screeching that erupts out in front of the house. Does she really think she can stop her father from leaving by acting feral?

One deep inhale and one slow exhale. I compose myself, straightening my tie one last time and smiling softly. The glass reflects a menacing grin. I blink and blink once more, for good measure. My reflection now matches the feel of my facial muscles, but the eyes in the glass are burning with an ominous glee. A jolt of shock stiffens my spine and I turn on my heel, hustling out to the hall as I remind myself, *That couldn't have been you.*

As expected, the party was an exercise in patience and flexing both my charm and restraint. Here I am now, dressed down and zoned out on Mom's new sectional. The hardwood floor feels smooth and cool under my stocking feet. It was a smart move on Mom's part to redo the flooring on the first story. Especially if my niece will be running wild around here indefinitely. Cleanup must be so much easier than it was with the polyester carpeting I grew up with. I wonder if Laura might convince Mom to repaint the cream-colored walls. Color would probably be much better at hiding the messes children make. My lips twitch in amusement as I picture Mom merely covering up any mishaps with yet another framed family picture. In my opinion, there's already so many more than necessary littered all throughout the typical common areas. My gaze drifts over Mom's prized hutch in the corner with her assorted knickknacks and memories made solid. I wonder how they will fare. My eyes stop on the television once more but don't take in whatever inane early evening sitcom is flashing on the screen. My train of thought hurtles back toward the party I just endured. So many times, I would have loved the opportunity to enact my fleeting fantasies of casual violence. Nothing makes my fingers itch to wrap around throats quite like the obligation to socialize with mundane, dull-minded suburbanites. Can they really be considered intrusive thoughts if you enjoy them?

A sudden shout of "Uncle Travis!" startles me out of my thoughts and doesn't even serve as a warning before a towheaded little monster plunges into my lap and starts pawing at me. The only thing that could make this worse would be if the kid had sticky hands. "Play with me," they whine. "I wanna play hide-n-seek!"

Thankfully, Laura appears quickly, though I'm still trying to compose my expression into something socially acceptable. Without missing a beat, she pulls her spawn off me and turns them to face her. Immediately, they wrap around her like an octopus and snuggle their face into her neck. She bends to kiss them gently atop their head and speaks softly but firmly near their ear. "I've told you already, leave Uncle Travis alone. He doesn't want to play, baby." Another kiss, and Laura sets them down on their feet. "I think Grandma is going to make cookies," she says slyly. "I saw her taking out her best cookie cutters."

Their doe-like eyes widen comically, and they let out a little gasp before spinning around and barreling toward the kitchen shouting, "Grammy, I wanna help!"

Rude though it may be, I can't help but shake my head in distaste. I don't know why my sister, or anyone, bothers to have children. "Thanks," I offer as an afterthought. I turn to see her watching me with a stiff smile. Unaffected as I am, the smile I return is much looser. Hovering, not sure if she really wants to sit with me, she tucks a stray strand of strawberry blond hair behind her ear and scratches the back of her earlobe—one of her tells.

I don't even attempt to shift my body language to make her more comfortable.

"I know we don't really talk much," she finally starts, "but I appreciate that you're here right now." Still unsure what to do with herself, she straightens the hem of her blouse and begins wringing her hands ever so subtly.

With an internal sigh, I grant her a bit of mercy. "At the end of the day, family is family." I get up and pull her into a hug. Her body relaxes only slightly, and I don't hold her very long. We pull apart with a fair bit of awkwardness on her part, and she excuses herself to go take a nap. I have no doubt she could use one. I'm very much looking forward to going to bed later, myself.

The sensation of weight shifting beside me and a hushed murmur near my ear coaxes me into consciousness, and I open my eyes to find I'm no longer alone in bed. There's no way I can truly be awake because my new bedmate is none other than the doppelgänger that's always peered out at me from every mirror I've ever looked into.

As I blink, desperate to get more light focused on my retinas, I notice this second self is not actually my exact twin. His hair, just a touch wavier than my own and kept an inch or so longer, is a deep chestnut rather than my own light auburn. His hazel eyes, boring into my own, are flecked with green instead of gold. There's something unsettling about his face—a nearly imperceptible malevolence etched deeply into every feature.

"You're—" My brain fails as his—my? our?—blunt fingernails ghost along my skin, down my sternum and back up toward the hollow of my throat, again and again. Of course, he'd know to touch me just like that. Even if I wanted to, I'd be unable to keep my eyelids from fluttering as a groan rises from the depths of my diaphragm.

He chuckles and presses himself closer against me. His skin feels amazingly warm and soft despite its appearance, pale and unyielding, like moonlight and the hard glass reflecting it.

"You're not me," I finally manage. My voice strains as his fingernail starts to lightly scratch down farther, toward my waistband. "I must be dreaming. Reflections don't come to life."

He circles my navel with that barely there touch and travels back up toward my throat. My skin flushes with warmth as blood rushes that much faster through my veins.

Another chuckle slips past his smirking lips as he gracefully shifts to sit up, straddling me. He captures my wrists and pins them up above my head. Usually, I'd be the one to pull such a

9

move, but I'm transfixed by the startling gaze that's somehow both strange and all my own. "Who said I was a reflection?" His voice is the same husky timbre I employ to seduce.

I'm just as susceptible to it as every former bedmate I've had the pleasure of knowing. My pupils expand, taking in the knowing edge to his sharpening grin.

"I'm a part of you, Travis." He pouts playfully as he adjusts to be better able to run a fingertip down my right oblique.

Another unstoppable groan escapes as I squirm.

"The part that you insist on running away from." He releases my wrists, and yet I stay frozen in place as he slowly comes down onto his forearms, pressing our bare chests together and brushing his lips against the side of my face.

I let out a shocked gasp and shudder at the puff of his breath against my skin. It's electrifyingly cool, like glass covered in morning dew.

"I'm done being ignored," he whispers in my ear. He nips at my earlobe, and I instinctively wrap my arms around him, letting out a soft hum of arousal as I roll my hips up against his. He laughs against me and presses his mouth to the side of my face. "It's time to accept me." He trails the curve of my jaw with more frisky nips, finally whispering against my parted lips. "Time to become who you're meant to be."

The deep, throaty laughter is coming from me now as I slip a hand up into his hair, wrapping the silky strands around my fingers. "And who am I meant to be?" I allow my eyelids to gently slide shut and sigh when he bears down with his pelvis, pressing me farther into the mattress.

He catches my lower lip between his teeth and tugs lightly. "Let me remind you," he mumbles. He bites down hard on the center of my lip, shifting the pressure from his front teeth to his canine. He cuts my pained gasp short by pressing our lips together, using his tongue to push the metallic taste of my own blood into my mouth.

I grip him more tightly as I surrender to the overwhelming tide of complete, perfect pleasure that I would only be able to get from myself. Our breaths synchronize as lips slide and tongues tangle together. As we thrust our hips together, I can feel the steady thrum of his pulse as if it were my own. While we seem to melt into each other, the memories flood my brain, firing off a fuzzy ecstasy through my nervous system. A stray spark of joy releases itself as a near cackle as I remember Jenny Tiller.

That first time I truly leaned into my instinctive callousness. I simply regurgitated and embellished stories about inverted men from upside-down houses that could never close their eyes and littered the rest of that night with warnings that those lidless eyes were always watching in the dark. All it took after that were a few well-timed growls just outside Laura's bedroom door, and Jenny was in tears as she all but ran out into the street and all the way home. She never did return to our house, and I manipulated my mother into turning a blind eye so easily. Knowing I had that power to hurt people—and even to get away with it—I felt godlike.

His voice interrupts my reminiscence. It's smooth and enticing, far in the back of my mind. *Remember the gerbil?*

Pride surges through me as I recall the memory, eliciting a happy moan.

It was so small, wasn't it? So warm and soft in your hands.

I feel my lips curve and curl smugly.

Wasn't it such a thrill to feel it struggle? Hear it squeak? Watch its eyes bulge when you finally gave it that last squeeze?

To this day, Mom and Laura think the pointless little rodent merely escaped, never to be found again.

Haven't you secretly wondered, all this time, how exquisite it would feel to play with people the same way?

Gasping as if I've just pulled myself up out of water, I throw my eyes open and blink the room into focus. Clean, cream walls with one artistically bland yet suitably pleasant landscape hung above the sturdy, plain desk. The old, worn drafting lamp sitting on the desk next to my laptop, and the squeaky office chair pushed in neatly. My suitcase laid down and open beside the unstained chest of drawers. Moonlight, unhindered by blinds or curtains, fills the room and gives the scene an ethereal feel. Nothing out of place and no longer anything extra. It's just me, but that's perfect.

I am here now, all of me, and I was exactly right. It's time to enjoy the life I've spent so many years denying myself.

My brain buzzes with excitement as I slip silently out of bed and cross over to pick out a fresh shirt and my favorite pair of lounging joggers. After all, I'm not a heathen. Being properly dressed lends my task a certain level of civility I much appreciate. Just as I reach out to grasp the knob and ease my door open, I hear it: the squeak of neglected hinges, followed by light but careless footfalls. They pass by my door, and moments later, I hear the click of a light switch. My niece, no doubt, needing the bathroom.

They seem such a delightful place to start.

THE WITCH

The stench hit her first. Her nostrils flared and her nose twitched pointlessly as hot, rancid decay burned through her nasal cavities and settled in her nasopharynx. Her stomach threatened to mutiny, and she dropped to the ground clutching her sides.

Next, the hair-raising chorus of hoarse voices crowded her mind with their inverse hymns, building upon each other until they grew as loud and chaotic as a sudden fracture in the earth. Her body trembled helplessly as the panic reached its crescendo, causing her blood to thunder through her veins, her head to spin, and her skin to glisten with a sweaty sheen.

An abrupt, sickening shriek—sounding like only a vague approximation of human— stabbed at her eardrums, and the claws descended. They shredded her clothing, ripped and tore her skin, attempted to pluck out her eyes. It seemed they would not stop until she lay in gruesome tatters on the cold, stone floor of the church.

Mary flung up in her bed with a tortured scream.

Her body shook. Her thin summer nightgown was soaked through with sweat, and her brain felt like an open wound. Carefully, she crept out of bed and turned on the light as quickly as possible. She glanced at the clock on the wall. Nearly one in the morning. She absently turned to her window—left ajar to keep the air fresh— and as if on cue, the memory of tolling bells echoed in her ears: The parish church bells, calling the faithful to come celebrate the birth of their savior. Or so she had thought once upon a time, when she'd suddenly found herself awake in the wee hours of Christmas morning.

"If only I'd not gone," she mumbled. She clapped her hands to her ears and dropped down to the floor, chin on her knees and back rigid against the wall. "If only I'd even thought to check the time." The bells rang louder in her head, and she slammed her eyes shut. "I'd have climbed right back into bed and gone back to sleep, and later, it would've seemed a dream."

Hot, desperate tears ran down to flavor the corners of her mouth with their saltiness. Her whole body felt fuzzy, as if the tolling of the iron bells reverberated against her skull. Just as she felt her eardrums might explode and her stomach might empty itself all over her bedroom floor, Mary let out an anguished cry and silence at last graced her weary mind.

It was still quite some time before Mary made a move. Once the horror of her nightmare and her memories subsided, leaving her with only a marrow-deep exhaustion, she stood and shuffled across the room and out the door. What she needed most just then was a soothing soak in the tub.

As the tub filled, she perched on the cushioned stool between it and the sink and allowed herself to think. That night, that one ill-fated Christmas, had changed her life forever. Of course, she could never set foot in church again, not after her narrow escape. That much had been clear when she'd seen the tattered remains of her best coat in Father Dunne's hands upon her arrival at the next Mass. That wasn't the only problem, nor was it the most pressing one. People had changed after that. Their perceptions had contorted into something dark and utterly hateful. People who had once called her *friend* now branded her *witch*.

Like every other time memory forced itself into her dreams—made her remember those dreadful, clutching claws and showed her the fate that had nearly befallen her—Mary thought of leaving. Moving to a new town, starting a new life. It was such a tempting, glorious thought. It filled Mary's heart with so much hope, but every time, her very next thought would crush the feeling into oblivion.

Where would I go? How would I get there? What's an old lady like me to really do?

Mary screamed again, this time in despondent frustration. She closed her eyes and dropped her face to rest in her upturned palms. Loath as she was to admit it, Mary was trapped. She had no one. No one who would welcome her with open arms to a new place. The only family she had, her husband and daughter, were both long buried in the parish graveyard.

An intrusive thought pounced on her then, one that had become startlingly familiar to her in recent months. As the warmth of the hot water radiated out from the tub, she gave the thought some real consideration.

What if I attended the Midnight Mass again? What more is there for me here, aside from hateful gossip, loneliness, and these ghoulish memories? As painful as it might be, to be torn to shreds, I'm sure it would all be over in the blink of an eye.

Her mind had wandered into this grisly, seemingly inevitable scenario only so far when she felt the air thicken around her. Prickles of unease pimpled her skin, and her muscles tensed with vigilance. Too frightened to see whatever ghastly phantom was surely materializing, she squeezed her eyes shut even tighter, until she could feel the tension of her skin tightening into furrows and deep creases across her forehead, along her nose, and near her eyes. Her hearing sharpened until the steady pouring of water into her tub more closely resembled a rushing waterfall, and her mind forced upon her the sensation of her own body dashed to pieces on a cluster of sharp, jagged rocks below.

Clutching at her throat, Mary sucked in a deep breath and forced herself to hold it for a count of ten. By the time she breathed back out, she had reassured herself that the thundering current in her head had actually been the anxious beating of her heart. As her breath evened, the sound calmed to a soft, soothing *shhhh*, and she opened her eyes, blinking a few times to sharpen her focus.

"Stop," she blurted. "Why do I keep thinking this way?" A prickling sense of awareness made the fine hairs along the nape of her neck and up her arms rise, despite the growing warmth of the room. "It's not right. I did nothing to deserve all this spite." Her eyes welled with tears as she recalled her dearest friend, Helen. It had been Helen's ghost who'd delivered the live-saving warning that night Mary mistakenly attended a Mass for the dead. It had been a breathtaking shock to turn around and find herself staring into a face she'd instantly recognized, despite its sallow, sunken appearance, but not so much as to keep Helen's urgent whisper from galvanizing her into action: "Leave now, before the hymn ends, and be quick."

Mary sprang up from her seat, standing tall and defiant. "Helen would be disgusted to see me treated this way." She nodded and chewed thoughtfully on the corner of her lower lip as she turned her attention back to the bath, which had filled up to her liking. *If only there were some way to fight back. If only Helen were here, she would have all sorts of ideas.* Coming up alongside the tub, Mary reached out to turn off the tap. *A steaming-hot bath is the best that can be done for now. It should help me sleep, at the least.* Just as she bunched up the front of her nightgown to pull it over her head, Mary spotted an odd sparkle under the water, right on the porcelain.

Bewilderment had her transfixed as she watched the speck expand into a gleaming length of gold that continued to stretch and morph until she found herself watching an elegant serpent rise along the side of the tub and poke its triangular head out of the water. A forked pink ribbon of a tongue darted out of its mouth, collecting information from the air.

A demented sob of laughter escaped as she realized not even the abrupt appearance of an impossible snake in her tub could truly faze her—not after what she had already experienced. Pulling together her thoughts, she noticed a subtle hiss slinking through the back of her mind. The snake almost seemed to smile as Mary snapped her jaw shut, cocked her head, and narrowed her eyes in questioning. She took the nearly imperceptible bow of its head as confirmation that it had infiltrated her very thoughts.

Dearessst, allow me to lead the way.

Mary staggered back. "Who?" She shook her head. "What are you?" A gasp leaped from her mouth as the only other place she had ever come across speaking serpents struck her. "The Devil!" She took another step back and crossed herself.

Light, lyrical laughter filled the room as the serpent disappeared, leaving in its place a fair-skinned, silver-haired woman stretched out comfortably in the bath. Their hooded eyes shone lilac, and the same golden serpent that had only just vanished coiled elegantly all the way up their left arm as a tattoo, the tip of its tail flirting with the lifeline in their palm and its jaw dropped, ready to strike at their shapely collarbone. "Call me Malik." They offered her a soft, close-lipped smile that turned the shrewdness of their face seductive. "I am something much older than all those lies."

Mary blinked rapidly and shook her head, stunned. "L—" She squinted at her unexpected guest, still lounging in the water as if she'd drawn the bath for them, and pushed out her question in a demanding tone. "Lies?"

"There is no such thing as the Devil." Malik stood and climbed out of the tub, small puddles forming at their feet as they took a moment to pull their long strands together and wring the water from the tips.

Mary watched them carefully, her wary mind cataloging details: smooth skin; light-colored moles of various sizes spread out over their pear-shaped body; a rounded, slightly protruding belly; a thick triangle of damp, coarse hair at their groin; and hairs so fine they would be practically invisible if not wet from the bath, just a bit too long to be stubble, running up from their ankles to mid-thigh. *Of course, the Devil would say such a thing*, she reasoned with herself, *and I know the Devil may take a pleasing shape, but...* Her eyes traveled back up and caught on their full breasts—which had just begun to sag with age—as they moved with Malik's breaths. Their noticeable unevenness stirred an inexplicable sense of kinship deep in Mary's core. *Surely, this is no devil. Just another woman, just like me.* She pulled her gaze farther up to see Malik watching her with a discerning expression and took a step back, momentarily startled by their intensity.

They approached Mary with a teasing curl to their plump lips, stopping close enough Mary had to fight her urge to take several steps back. Being only inches apart from each other in height made it impossible for Mary not to stare directly into their bright eyes. It was a feeling akin to being hypnotized, and it kept her from realizing Malik had reached out until the touch of their long, slender finger dragged from the hollow of her throat to the tip of her chin. She couldn't stop the shiver of unexpected pleasure that trailed up her spine in tandem with the faint scratch of their fingernail.

Malik's voice dropped to a sultry purr, and they continued, "The Devil's merely a fantasy spoon fed to you by generations of men in stiff white collars terrified of their own desires."

Mary's pulse picked up, and she unconsciously swept the tip of her tongue across her lips. "And why are you here?" The subtle sting of her nails digging into her palms as she curled her fingers inward kept her calm enough to continue boldly. "What would you have from me?"

Mischief broke out across Malik's face, the lilac of their irises seeming to glow. "What exactly would you believe?" they asked in a playful tone that betrayed just how little they truly cared.

"I suppose it doesn't really matter, does it?" Mary shifted, bringing her arms up to cross them over her chest. She began to worry at her lip again as she regarded Malik curiously.

They gave the slightest nod, agreeing with her assessment. "As far as this village is concerned, you're already damned." The impression of a sympathetic smile flashed across their face when Mary sucked in a breath and looked away.

"As far as you're concerned, it seems you already have your heart set on the grave." They abruptly grasped Mary by the shoulders, surprising her into locking gazes once again. Mary tensed in surprise but quickly relaxed when she caught the playfulness in Malik's eyes and the way they bit back a laugh. "So why not entertain me? Together, we can sow a little chaos." A sweet, imploring smile spread across their face as they moved in closer and brought their hands up from her shoulders to lovingly cup her face. "I'll make it worth your while, dearest. I can provide you with vengeance." They moved closer still, now wrapping Mary up in a comforting hug that she easily fell into and reciprocated. Her nightgown dampened as it pressed against Malik's still-wet skin, and she shivered. Goose bumps rose on her skin when they brushed their lips along her cheek on their way to whisper into her ear. They softened their tone to a delicate murmur. "Surely, sister, that would be more pleasurable than to die in brutal agony as the dead rend you apart."

Mary shivered, part in revulsion at the gruesome image that jumped to mind and part due to having gone so long without any form of positive touch. It elicited within her a strange mixture of comfort, trust, and arousal. She hugged Malik tighter, pressing her fingers into the bare, cool flesh of their back and letting her eyes fall shut. She let out a happy moan when she felt their fingers move through her hair.

"Yes," she sighed. Mary's lips curved up into a shape she had convinced herself they no longer knew how to make, turning her face into a map of fine lines and creases. Slowly, feeling as if she were in a dream, she pulled away just far enough to see Malik's face. As they peered into each other's eyes, a vindictive glee crept across Mary's features. "Help me, and I'll gladly be this town's witch."

THE SPURNED CHILD

Mistake.

The word swelled in his mind, dripped down his spinal cord, and finally simmered low in his gut.

Mistake.

It twisted and thrashed, struck out like a snake trying to protect itself, and poisoned his blood.

"*Mistake,*" he scoffed and, after a while, opened his mouth to share his thoughts with his reflection on the surface of the water. "My love is not a mistake."

His ethereal eyes glowed with unbridled resentment. "Pride? Ha! Father just couldn't face the ferocity of my loyalty." He sneered, turning his glorious features utterly menacing. "He doesn't *understand* love."

After staring at himself for another long moment, he nodded and practically flung himself to his feet. "Fine. If *that's* how he wants it, I'll just have to make him regret turning me out." The solution dawned on him, filling him with a caustic joy. "If I'm to believe anything that's ever come out of his mouth, then there's nothing that hurts him more than having to teach his beloved children a lesson." His lips curved into a smug little smirk. "Whatever could his new little doll be up to right now?" He set off to find out.

He found her in a laughably ideal spot—under his favorite tree. She idly ran her delicate, slender fingers through her fine hair as she eyed the low-hanging fruit with open curiosity. He came up alongside her and smiled cheerfully.

"Hello, Eve."

APPOINTED GUARDIAN

SATURDAY, OCTOBER 11TH

There was a way to contact your guardian angel.

Sarah had heard it from Mandy, who had heard it from her brother.

"A bunch of them were whispering about it last Sunday, at reception," Mandy confided. They been huddled so closely together at the farthest, loneliest edge of the courtyard that Mandy's brother hadn't noticed her walking up to them with a Dixie cup of lemonade and half a glazed donut. She'd been able to get the full story out of him later that evening, but there was no knowing if he'd told her the truth or had changed up details just to scare her.

When they heard about the blood required, Sarah felt just as doubtful as Mandy. It all sounded a bit more like spirit communication and a lot less like prayer, and when Sarah really thought about it, their father's disapproving grumble echoed in their head: *Sounds like witchcraft and Satan to me.*

Sarah sent the letter all the same, so they could know for sure.

Pricking their finger with a sewing needle was surprisingly scary, but Sarah managed. They made sure to puncture deep enough to let two bright crimson beads drip down right onto the paper before popping their finger into their mouth and mindlessly pressing their tongue against it until it stopped hurting. Once the blood dried, they folded the letter up, placed it in a plain, unstamped, unaddressed envelope, and waited. Setting their alarm clock was not an option. With the shrill racket it made, the entire household would stir. It was easier for Sarah to feign sleep for the in-between hours. Midnight came sooner than anticipated, and anxious excitement buzzed just under their skin, pimpling their flesh as they slipped out from under their covers. Quiet as their mother always expected them to be whenever *the men* were talking, they crept out of the house. They went down to the corner, turned right onto Line Street, and walked until they reached the public mailbox over by Mandy's house, where they dropped the letter before heading back home.

Sarah had written a simple message. *Please, I need a friend. Love, Tom.*

THURSDAY, OCTOBER 30TH

Sarah huddled into themself, propping their elbows up on the ceramic tile counter of the cutout that separated the kitchen from the living room, and lowered their voice. "You know I can't—"

31

There was a pointed cough from their father, and Sarah immediately corrected themself with a frown.

"You know I don't go trick-or-treating." Sarah wanted to add that they appreciated the offer but quickly thought better of it. "You really should stop asking me," they said instead, making sure their voice carried clearly. Listening to their friend's response, they tugged anxiously at the telephone cord. "Yeah, alright. See you in English." They stole a quick glance toward their parents at the dining room table. "Bye, Nolan."

Their father huffed disapprovingly as Sarah came back to their spot at the table. "I think you should stop associating with that boy." He leveled a stern look at them, and Sarah was able to hold his gaze only briefly before shifting to look down at the table. "He wants to lead you astray."

Sarah's mother responded in a meek, conciliatory tone. "Rob, honey. Let's not get carried away now. He's just a lost boy. He's not *trying* to cause any harm." She reached out to grab a pamphlet from the neat, orderly stacks of three-by-five gospel comics she'd gotten through Pastor Jones and slipped the Chick Tract into a goody bag with a couple of Dum Dums.

Robert took back control of the conversation before she could add on anything else. "I tell you one thing, Deborah. There's something wrong with that boy." He shook his head as he shoved a completed bag away, toward the far end of the table, and grabbed an empty one. "How long have we allowed him to be friends with our Sarah? And he's not shown any interest? A healthy boy should be looking for a girlfriend at his age." He spared a glance in Sarah's direction and snorted. "He must be one of those queers!" His face flushed and he sat taller in his chair, knocking his fist against the tabletop indignantly. "Only to be expected," he pushed on in a tone not unlike their pastor during a particularly impassioned sermon. "When a boy is raised without a father." He thrust his pointer finger up in the air, shaking it at his wife and daughter in turn. "Single mothers make soft little boys, not strong, respectable men."

Sarah kept their body loose and their expression blank as they avoided their father's gaze and mechanically grabbed a Chick Tract.

Deborah reached out and squeezed his shoulder soothingly. "We're a good influence for him, Robert," she asserted in a hushed, slow voice. She moved her hand up to stroke the back of Robert's neck. His shoulders eased down from around his ears, and the ruddiness left his cheeks.

"A good girl like Sarah is just the kind of friend he needs." Deborah turned a proud maternal smile over to them and winked. "And if a romance blooms, think of what a glorious testimony it will be!"

Robert sighed deeply and closed his eyes, taking one more moment of comfort from his wife's touch before he shrugged, cuing her to take her hand away and go back to filling trick-or-treat bags. "You're right. Of course you're right." He blinked his eyes open and gave Sarah a sheepish smile. "I'm sorry, baby girl." He reached out and put his hand atop theirs, patting it briefly. "It's just all this"—he gestured to the loosely sorted piles on the dining table: twist ties and empty goody bags, opened bags of cheap candy, and the Chick Tracts—"it puts me in such a sour mood."

Sarah could understand that, at least. Halloween always made them especially anxious. Things had improved once Deborah finally succeeded in convincing Robert that concessions had to be made to secularism. Sarah no longer had to help him get toilet paper out of the tree outside their bedroom window or clean all the egg and shell off the garage door, but they paid in the way he needed to be treated with kid gloves all throughout October.

"You catch more flies with honey," Deborah reminded in the placating, singsong voice she often used with him. She smiled to herself as she put down another impeccably assembled treat bag.

"It just feels too much like paying a blackmailer," Robert grumbled, "or negotiating with terrorists. It's a damned shame we have to give any kind of acknowledgment to such a satanic holiday!" He gave a violent, huffing snort and shook his head again. "This country is really going to Hell in a handbasket, the way Halloween is getting to be such a big deal."

Sarah quickly bore down on their lower lip with their right canine to hold back the heavy sigh that wanted to escape and to fight the impulse to apologize for something that wasn't their fault.

The three of them continued prepping what Deborah preferred to call *Gospel Bags* in silence. *At least it'll be over and done with tomorrow*, Sarah reassured themself. Not for the first time that day, they wondered if their brother celebrated Halloween, out in the world and free from parental scrutiny, and felt a bitter pang of jealousy knowing they'd never be allowed to go to college. They had to hold in another sigh.

Eamon paused for a moment, reading the house. Ten Pike Street—a single story craftsman—sat unassumingly behind immaculate flower beds and a meticulously maintained yard graced by a dogwood tree sporting fiery red leaves. Its modest taupe exterior, remarkably clean white accents and trim, and well-swept welcome mat seemed to broadcast a message of peace and familial harmony. *A den of deceit*, Eamon surmised. They turned their attention back to the imploring tug of blood that had led them here. The pull was strongest near the first bedroom, the one that looked out onto the street. As desperately as it called to them, Eamon kept moving. Down the foyer, past the second bedroom that emanated no signs of life, past a dining table, and through the living room into the primary suite. They were curious about the other humans that lived here.

Robert and Deborah slept, oblivious to the late-night visitation. Robert's snores filled the room with a harsh, discordant sort of music. He lay starfished across the bed, a thin line of drool escaping out the side of his open mouth. Eamon could stand to look at him only so long and threw their attention to Deborah. A sense of tragedy overtook them as they considered her, crammed along the edge of the bed, her face as blank as the feeling that came from her. Having sensed all they needed to know, Eamon turned back to the rest of the house and finally made their way to Sarah's room.

They paused at the bedside, taking in everything they could as Sarah slept with a soft, peaceful expression on their face and their hands tucked up under their cheek, as if in prayer. Sarah's lips were loose and relaxed, letting out soft breaths that shifted the stray strands of ashy brown hair that had fallen over their face. A band of light freckles scattered from one cheek to the other, and their lashes fanned out across their fair skin like little dark ribbons of silk. The moonlight filtering in through the slanted blinds bathed them in a gentle light that only enhanced Sarah's innocence, and Eamon decided their mission was to protect this human child with all their strength. They fashioned themself a corporeal form so they could sweetly brush the hair from Sarah's face and rest a hand on their forehead. "I have come, child."

Sarah stirred slightly as they began to dream under Eamon's watchful eye.

Tom found himself drenched in darkness, clutching at his own elbows, and shivering in the unnatural chill. He blinked twice, to clear the haze from his brain, and waited for his eyes to adjust. "*If* they adjust," he huffed. To his relief, things began to take shape within his field of vision, and he soon realized that he stood in the shadows of an empty alleyway. "Okay, so obviously, I'm dreaming." He confirmed by patting his chest and noting the absence of developing breasts. His dreams were the only place where he didn't have to force himself to fit the pinching, biting confines of being Sarah. "Well, this is new. Where on earth am I?" Not fully trusting what little he could see, he groped about until his hand met brick and used that to guide himself along. "Thank God," he muttered when the alley suddenly opened up. The silvery light of the moon and stars exposed an empty city street. He turned right onto the cobbles and walked on, ignoring the cheap, cardboard look of the buildings. The air seemed to heat up the tiniest degree as he moved, just enough to keep him from dropping to the ground so he could huddle into himself for warmth.

"Hello," he called out after walking for what felt like miles. "Where is everybody? I know someone's here!" An involuntary shiver racked his body. "I can feel you watching me!" The staged buildings had disappeared some time ago, replaced by a gaping, infinite nothing on either side of the cobblestones under his feet. "This has gotta be the most bogu—" Tom stopped short, nearly tripping over himself, when he spotted what looked like a child on the side of the road, just a little way ahead. His curiosity and concerned confusion morphed into terror the closer Tom got. *Totally heinous*, he thought as he took in tattered rags hanging loose on a pale, scabby and scared, emaciated little body. One corner of his lip was curling up in a disturbed grimace when the stranger abruptly turned to face him. The scream that wanted to claw its way up his larynx and explode from his mouth was stuck, sitting in his chest like heartburn. His legs trembled but firmly refused to carry Tom away as the sightless ghoul approached, its void-like eye sockets trained on him. Once it was close enough to reach out and touch Tom, it stopped and raised its withered face.

"Lend me your light," it suggested in an ambiguous, genderless voice far too old for its childlike stature.

That overrode every command Tom's brain had been trying to send to his body, and he found himself slowly lowering into a squat, his left hand resting on his left knee and his right hand splaying out against the cold ground to help him retain his balance. His pulse quickened, rushing through his veins and booming in his head like cannon fire. Droplets of sweat formed at his temples, and his throat constricted in panic as the creature's hands reached up and those skeletal fingers came closer and closer to Tom's eyes. He tried frantically to slam his eyelids shut, but to no avail. He could only stare, wide-eyed, as fingertips began to press against him.

To his utter astonishment, it did not hurt. There was simply an odd, slightly uncomfortable pressure as those fingers forced their way in over his lower lid and scooped under his eyeballs. Then came more insistent pressure, this time in the other direction and, along with the disquieting sound of tearing and popping, two short, sharp tugs that were over before his brain could decide he was in pain.

"You will not want these," stated his grotesque little guide. "Not to talk to the angel."

"Th-the angel?" Tom was interrupted by a soft squelch, and somehow, he knew the creature had just popped his eyeballs into its own empty sockets.

"I will keep them safe. Now stand and take my hand, child."

Tom did as commanded, sensing how the thing he'd assumed was a child had suddenly grown tall enough to reach down for his hand and gently pull him forward. As they moved along, the air continued to warm until Tom felt the pleasant drowsiness of a perfect day on the cusp of summer. The freshly mutilated sockets that previously housed his eyes still felt the searing brightness of a mighty light, and he was glad to have been shielded from it. An energizing sense of awe tugged at the deepest parts of his soul, and he felt uplifted. *This must be what church is supposed to feel like*, he thought as a light, airy sigh escaped him.

There was the rustling of wings, and then a voice came creeping toward him from all sides, its multiple layers of young and old, gendered and genderless, human and inhuman like waves lapping at the shore. "Tom, my child." The voices all met together and settled into one eerily quasi-human tone as it continued. "I have followed your blood. I am Eamon, and I will visit righteous wrath upon the nonbelievers."

Tom shivered in a mix of fear and instinctive reverence. Then, Eamon's words fully registered and he staggered back a step. "Nonbelievers?" He shook his head in bewilderment. "You mean my parents? But they're—they *are* believers!"

Eamon tsked. "The woman is emptied, mindless. She is a doll manipulated willingly and seeks only to produce more of her ilk. The man overflows with greed and malice. He lusts after control and defames the Lord."

Tom wanted to protest. He desperately wanted to be able to argue, but he simply couldn't counter the truth. Instead, he tried to appeal to Eamon's sense of mercy.

"But wrath? You mean— You'll *kill* them?"

A blast of sweltering heat burst forth, leaving him feeling singed, though a quick pat down of his arms assured him his body was unharmed.

"They will be judged for their mockeries," Eamon roared, their voice separating once again into myriad layers of rage.

Tom's knees nearly buckled as he was engulfed by the fervent desire to drop to the ground and beg forgiveness, but a bony hand on his shoulder stilled him.

"Strength," advised his creature guide in a soothing whisper. "The angel will do no harm to the innocent."

A new thought struck him, and Tom stammered as he collected his nerve. "B-but Eamon. I-I'm just a kid. I can't be left alone. It's not— It's against the law. I need a guardian." He chewed nervously on his lower lip and offered his vulnerability. "Also, I don't want to be left alone. Please, Eamon. Please, don't do this and leave me all alone."

A cool, refreshing breeze caressed his face, and the brightness stinging Tom's eye sockets seemed to lessen for a moment, putting him at ease. "Fear not, my son. You will not be abandoned."

The cozy heat radiating out alongside Eamon's light began to dissipate, and Tom felt himself being guided downward.

"Rest now."

The cold enveloped him like an icy cocoon as his back flattened against the ground.

"I will return and all will be just."

As Tom succumbed to the chill, Eamon vanished, and Sarah fell into a deep, dreamless sleep.

FRIDAY, HALLOWEEN NIGHT

Robert paced irritably as Deborah and Sarah worked together to clear the table, then wash, dry, and put away the dishes. "It's almost time," he snapped. "Any minute now, those little heathens will start ringing our bell, demanding candy." He paused to breathe in deeply and let the breath back out in one forceful, loud huff. "And we'll have to smile and tell them what little sweethearts they are in their little costumes." He stopped again, sneering at no one in particular, though he was facing his wife and daughter. "Those older kids these days, dressing up as pop stars. Idolatry," he spat. "Idolatry right on my doorstep!"

Deborah handed Sarah the last dish to dry and flocked over to her husband, stroking his neck and shoulders. "Now now, honey." She went up onto the balls of her stocking feet and kissed his cheek. "Let's not get ourselves into a knot over this. It'll be over soon." She ran her fingers along his jaw and down the side of his throat, melting the lines of tension in his face.

Sarah finished up in the kitchen and started looking through the cabinets for a big enough bowl.

"This is important work we do," Deborah cooed, "witnessing with the Gospel Bags. What better night to spread God's message than . . ." She trailed off, her fingers going limp and her hands dropping away from Robert.

"Deborah?" His body tensed in concern and his heart seized, sending a jolt of pain and raw, frigid dread through his body. Cold sweat dotted his hairline as he caught his wife in his arms just before she crumpled to the floor. "Debbie!" He whipped his head up, toward the kitchen. "Sarah," he barked, "your mother! Call 911!"

He didn't bother to make sure she'd followed his direction, too busy reading Deborah's face for clues. Her mouth dropped open, as if her jaw had unhinged, and she emitted a shrill shriek. Unwilling to let go of his wife, Robert squirmed in agony, waiting for his eardrums to burst and clenching his jaw against the confused scream he didn't want to let out. Just as quickly as she had begun, Deborah stopped screeching. Her mouth snapped violently shut with a loud *clap*, followed by a sickening *crunch*.

"Debbie?" Robert blinked away tears and cautiously caressed her brow, brushing hair out of her face as he continued to hold her. "Sweetheart?" The corners of her mouth slickened with blood-tinged drool. "My wife," he worried in a tiny, petrified whimper. "My beautiful wife. What's happening?"

His eyes bulged and he let out a grunt as Deborah's eyelids stretched open impossibly wide and her green-flecked hazel irises seemed to fracture and expand. "What in God's name?" His pulse slammed in his ears, and sweat rolled down his neck, soaking the collar of his shirt. Before his eyes, Deborah's scleras seemed to bubble and boil, until they hissed and crackled like a foil of Jiffy Pop on the stove. Finally, with one last gut-churning *pop* that reverberated in Robert's head, her eyes exploded, sending wet chunks of organ meat though the air. He shouted in disgust and threw her body to the floor. The back of her head made a horrific *crack* against the vinyl flooring of the dining room. Blood began to seep out from underneath her like searching fingers.

"No," Robert howled and dropped down, not even noticing the sharp pain of his knees slamming against the floor. He crawled to straddle his wife's still body, sobbing openly as he reached up and cradled her face in his shaking, sweaty hands. "What have I done?" He leaned down and pressed his wet, snotty lips to hers. "Please," he whispered against them. "Please, God. I'm sorry, just, please. My wife." He repeated himself, turning the words into a prayer as he closed his eyes and willed God to notice his torment.

Deborah's mangled eye sockets began to glow with a blinding brightness that washed out the whole room like a flashbulb, and her mouth twitched, drool-soaked lips separating and broken teeth making an unsettling sound as they ground together. Robert sprang back, kneeling astride her, and sucked in a few shallow, wavering breaths as he squinted against the light. "Deborah?"

She tilted her head, directing her blistering gaze right at his face. The air punched out of his lungs in a harsh, painful gasp as his own eyes began to sizzle.

"Charlatan!" A bone-chilling fury leaped from Deborah's mouth in a voice not her own as her hand whipped up and caught Robert by the throat hard enough to make his eyes bulge. He found himself held up in the air, dangling helplessly and struggling for breath in his wife's viselike grip. She herself was somehow suspended several feet off the ground, her mouth an angry slash of ruined teeth, blood-matted hair clinging to the sides of her face. Those blinding shallows that once held eyes continued to bore into his, making them cook and burn faster, until they turned to ash and Robert wheezed in misery. His mouth flopped open and shut stupidly as he struggled to form sounds beyond labored breaths.

"You butcher the Divine and defile the love of Christ," Deborah accused in an animalistic growl. His windpipe crushed and his spine snapped as she tightened her grip on his neck, yet he did not die. Every neuron in his brain pleaded for the mercy of death, but something kept him alive and conscious. The only grace he could enjoy was his inability to see the ghastly beast his wife had become. Relying only on the feel of her and the sound of this voice that had never belonged to her before, he could almost convince himself it wasn't, in fact, *his* Deborah doing these ghoulish things to him.

An abrupt pain made his heart clench, and he wished he could cry out. A molten heat plunged into his gut and shot up through his esophagus, down through his intestines, and all through his veins. His brain now wailed for death, but still, it didn't come.

"Your kind preaches often about a lake of fire," Deborah hissed, "so I shall let you burn even beyond the end of days."

Outside the humble little craftsman, with its clean trim and spectacular red-leaved tree, Halloween was finally underway. The first, early groups of eager trick-or-treaters were beginning to stream down Pike Street.

It was just as a gaggle of little ghosts, fairies and clowns, and some teenaged Madonnas and Boy Georges started up the walkway to Ten Pike Street that the house seemed to explode into an almost blinding pillar of unearthly fire that reached up to the heavens, all with an unnerving, unnatural silence. Parents that had fallen behind raced to grab their children and yank them away as they shielded their young eyes. The teenagers stood rooted to the spot, unable to tear their squinted gazes away as others screamed in shocked disbelief. It took hardly any time at all for the trick-or-treaters to realize the flames were not spreading beyond the house and that no blazing, burning heat licked at their feet or seared their skin. As the crowd gathered around with gaping mouths and candy-filled pillowcases slack at their sides, a form emerged from the flames.

Tom stepped out from his home, holding his mother's largest mixing bowl out in front of him. Goody bags were piled high, threatening to spill out over the sides. His mother followed shortly after, looking as composed and pleasant as ever, but moving in awkward jerks like a marionette being manipulated by a new, unskilled puppeteer. As she came to a stilted stop on the last porch step, the soundless inferno behind her was extinguished, as if it had never been, and the house stood exactly as it had before. Tom continued down the walk to meet the crowd where they stood and greeted them all with a welcoming grin. He squatted down until he was eye level with the smallest trick-or-treaters and held out the bowl encouragingly.

"What do you say?" he asked in a bright, cheerful voice.

DEATHWISH

She's like the morning light as it slowly fills your bedroom, exposing dancing dust motes and warming the air. Even better: she's a quickly retreating dream that leaves you hazy, wanting, and grasping.

She's just so pale, you see. A creamy alabaster tone that makes me think of luscious white chocolate melting in my mouth. She's no Snow White with bloody lips and midnight hair. Instead, chestnut hair feathers down past her shoulders, only a shade or two off from her sweet brown eyes. Her full lips, unglossed—a peachy pink, with an exquisitely formed cupid's bow up top. Whenever she bats her eyes at me, and that tantalizingly rosy blush colors the apples of her cheeks, I think my heart might stop.

"Come with me," she urges in that sultry tone.

A fit of violent, hacking coughs rouses me. My own. I try desperately to hold them in, but of course, my malnourished body is not up to the task. I can only try not to cry at the agonizing, dry scrape of my throat and the heaving lurching of my lungs as I cough and cough and cough. It continues until I'm too weakened to do anything but slip back into sleep. That's okay, though. I'd rather sleep my life away than face this rotting, war-torn reality.

In dreams, I still have clean, white blinds and a warm bed in a cozy room full of lazy motes drifting in the soft, pale light that is just like her. When I dream, I can dream of her, and how she'll take me away from all this. I can believe, then, that she is coming.

An unearthly cry echoes through the looted, plague-ridden streets and fills the rancid rooms of these decrepit houses. It pulls me into the waking world, and I lie still with my eyes still closed, listening to screams as they rise up. That's when I realize—that first cry was the neigh of a horse. I can hear the pounding clomp of its hooves as it advances. The wails grow louder, mingle with the sounds of struggle and panic.

I muster the last remnants of my strength to pull myself up and hobble to the space where there once was a front door. I make it only as far as the curb of the cracked sidewalk before my body crumples under me and I erupt in more excruciating coughs. I force myself to keep my eyes open through the pain and focus down the street.

A great steed, larger than even a shire, pale as fresh, pristine snow. No, paler. So pale that the animal seems to glow, with a ghostly white mane and tail, and all-white leather trappings. On its back, she is there. My exquisite, pale death.

It's almost so funny as to be sad, watching people as sick and starving as me attempt to run. Not only is it a stupid idea, to think you can flee the Horseman, it's ludicrous. An absurd proposition. Instead of being a Godforsaken fool like the others, I force my body out into the streets, into the rider's path, and clasp my hands in a twisted parody of prayer.

"Please," I scream as loud as my hoarse voice can manage. "Take me."

Anything is better than continuing to live through the Apocalypse.

HOSTILE TAKEOVER

I've always been just a little too weak while you were still a little too strong. The farthest I've managed to go is the darkest, most obscure corner in the back of your mind, and it was only for the briefest of rides. It was long enough, though. Long enough to know that you're the one, and tonight is the night I finally succeed.

Your nighttime routine is titillating, as always. Watching your hands glide over all that bare, supple skin under the showerhead has me raw with want. I can't wait to have control over something. It's been far too long since I've enjoyed the pleasure of flesh.

You managed to fall asleep as I watched from the shadows, but it was clearly a struggle. You sense my presence these days, more strongly than before. It doesn't matter, though. Not now that you've woken up to find your body immovable. All you can do is blink away tears and try your best to even out your short, shallow breaths as your throat constricts and your brain seems to swell and press against the inside of your skull.

I can feel the shrieking along your synaptic bridges as I make myself at home, a frenzied hum of commands your body refuses to follow. It's a pleasant, ticklish buzz to me, but all the same, I loosen the reins just a bit. I am curious what you might have to say to me.

"Is this possession?" Your voice is small and frightened.

Almost there, I reply as I wrap myself around your brainstem. *Almost mine*.

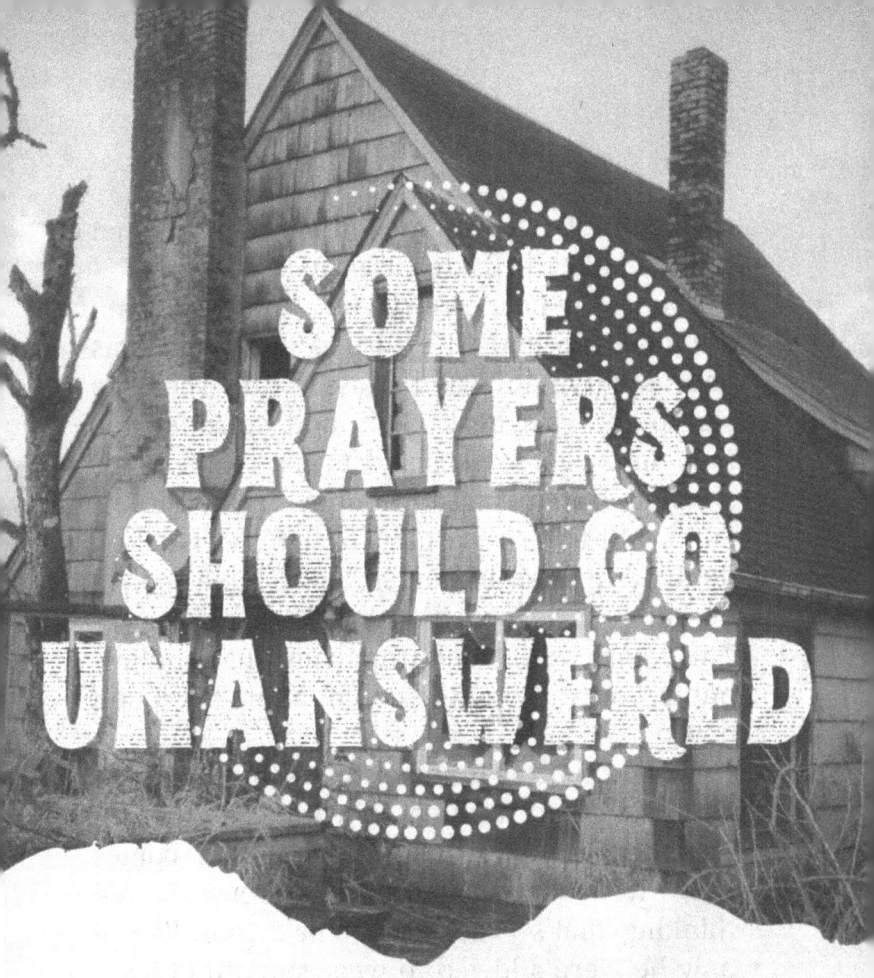

SOME PRAYERS SHOULD GO UNANSWERED

A gentle, cool breeze drifted in through the open window, shifting the sheer, lace-frilled curtains that served form over function. Playful shrieks erupted—clearly the Thompson twins from two houses over, playing tag in their backyard. There was the slam of a car door, followed by excited barks from what sounded like the Dachshunds next door.

"Mrs. Spencer must be home," Devon mumbled absently. He turned away from his bedroom window and crossed the room to slump into his desk chair and consider the porcelain figurine he held in his hand: a fair skinned, flaxen haired little boy dressed in his Sunday Best. A rosary hung from his wrist like a doubled-up bracelet, and he held a bible open in his hands as he looked up with his big, doe eyes. The colors were faded from constant handling, but Devon still saw the doll in all its fresh and new glory.

He had spotted it in the store some years ago now, and had wanted it with the kind of inexplicable, inflexible fierceness that comes easy to young children. He remembered thinking that's exactly what he'd look like, if only he were allowed to wear suits to Church. Always the softer touch, his mother had seen no problem with indulging him. His father, on the other hand, had stiffened as he often did when he was digging his heels in for a fight. Devon could still see the flush of ruddy red that had bloomed on his cheeks as he'd turned to look his wife straight in the eye.

"Absolutely not," he'd ordered in a low voice. Devon's chest tightened as his body momentarily relived the peculiarly heart-wrenching sense of disappointment he'd felt. He thought he could feel the ghost of the tears that had formed back then. Blinking, he realised that his eyes really were tearing up, and he held the doll tighter. The barely contained irritation and shame that had saturated his father's tone echoed in Devon's head as he recalled the words "Enough, Lindy. Enough. It's time Devon drop this tomboy nonsense, and it's time we stop treating it like a harmless stage she'll grow out of. Look at how confused she is."

Devon sniffled as he remembered trying to run out of the store. Pulling in a deep breath through his nose, he forced himself to swivel in his chair and put the doll away in its place next to the framed family photo that sat obscuring the clamp of his Architect lamp. His gaze instinctively shifted over to the matching figurine shoved off to the far corner of the desktop, covered in a layer of dust and in danger of falling off at any moment. That had been the compromise, once his parents had managed to calm him down. He could have the figurine he wanted, but only if he got its mate.

Another high, shrill scream from the direction of the Thompson house served as the perfect commentary when a cramp tore through

Devon, making him hunch forward and hold his abdomen as he dropped his head down atop the bible open on his desk. He whimpered pathetically, overcome with the merciless reality.

Puberty was coming for him, as sure and fearsome as The Day of Reckoning.

The persistent, throbbing pain that sat deep and low in his abdomen was now familiar. He'd insisted *my tummy hurts, that's all* for as long as he could, until the bone-deep weariness had begun to creep up on him as well, his chest had begun to swell and ache, and even his very skin had felt different. His mother's misty-eyed smile and the loving pride in her soft voice every time she hugged Devon close and whispered "You're becoming a woman" was a red-hot poker straight to his heart as he hid his face against her chest and clung to the fact that she loved him. Anytime she kissed the top of his head, cooing "anytime now," he squeezed his eyes tighter to keep his tears inside.

I can't stop God's plans, he ruminated. *I can't stop a girl body from doing what it does.* He bit the inside of his cheek and grunted in resentment when the pain failed to distract him from the apparent riot in his abdomen. *I can try one last time, though*, he asserted with another grunt. *Mom and Dad love me. They've gotta understand, they've gotta accept me.* Letting himself focus on the suburban soundscape outside his window, Devon breathed deeply and evenly until the cramps subsided. "They love me." His voice was firm and insistent he sat up. "It'll be okay." He eyed his bible and the daily devotional journal he'd been gifted for the summer. "I just gotta try a different approach."

He found his mother in the living room, indulging in her guilty pleasure soap opera as she did the ironing. "Mom?" He paused just inside the room, offering her the kind of meek smile that both his parents loved best. He waited until she rested her iron and returned his smile with a tender one of her own. "Can we talk about my devotional?"

Her eyes sparkled as her smile widened. "Of course, Sweetheart. I love talking Scripture with you!" She looked around for the TV remote while Devon came to perch anxiously on the edge of the couch. Locating the remote, she muted the television and made herself comfortable on one end of the couch. "Devon, you're miles away. Come closer, I promise I won't bite," she teased.

Sighing, Devon scooted closer to her, but remained on the edge, turning his body in towards her, so they could look each other in the eye, and opening his bile up on his lap. "Well," he hedged, "ummm." He flipped the delicate, tissue-thin bible pages between his fingers as he forced himself to maintain eye contact. He tried distracting himself from the flush he felt creeping up his neck and the cool clamminess of his hands that was beginning to make the bible pages stick by focusing on the warm amber of his mother's eyes. He'd always found the softness of her gaze comforting. Finally, he continued. "I was reading Psalms 139."

"Oh, I love that one," she interjected excitedly. She reached out and patted his hand. "Did you find any one verse especially impactful?"

"Uh, yeah," he chuckled awkwardly and jerked his gaze down to his bible. He traced the lines with his pointer finger as he read aloud. "For You formed my inward parts; You covered me in my mother's womb." He skipped ahead a verse and continued. "My frame was not hidden from You, when I was made in secret, *and* skillfully wrought in the lowest parts of the earth."

He tilted his face back up to see her openly beaming in pride and she brushed the hair out of his face, tucking it back behind his ears. "Such beautiful words," she said. "That Psalm always makes me think of when I was pregnant." She rubbed her own belly. "When He knit you together in my womb."

Devon couldn't help but smile back at her, despite his nerves. *See, she loves you so much. It'll be fine.*

"So, Baby, what do you think those verses mean?"

Devon closed his bible and set it between them on the couch. He pretended to think for a long beat. "I think," he flashed her a smile, "it's saying that He knew who I would be. Even before you got pregnant, He knew I'd be Devon and He knew how He wanted Devon to be formed." He paused, basking in the growing pride that jumped out at him from his mother's bright eyes. "I think God knows everyone's soul from before they were even born because He made every one of them just how He wanted them to be, and He makes no mistakes."

She threw her arms up, palms upturned, and practically shouted, "Amen." She leaned in and gave him a peck on the forehead. "You're exactly right, my brilliant girl!"

Another apprehensive chuckle flew out past his lips, and he subtly tried to create some distance by sitting back and letting himself sink slightly as the well-loved couch sagged under him. "Well, then, Mom." He gave himself a moment. *Be strong, Devon. You can't let your voice break.* He couldn't meet her eye anymore and settled for focusing on the small beauty mark just under her right eye. He sat up as straight as the sagging cushions would allow him and threw his shoulder back. "Why is it so hard to believe I'm a boy?" He looked directly into her eyes for a fraction of a second before focusing on the mole again. "H—He made me this way. He knew what he was doing. He knit me together this way, as a boy in a girl body." Finished, he dared to meet her gaze again and shrunk in on himself as he watched a spark of anger morph into a deep, fearful pity that seemed to darken the brown of her irises and deepen the wrinkles in her face.

"Oh, you poor thing." She rushed forward and wrapped her arms around him, forcing him to move closer, until she was clutching him to her chest, and he was halfway sitting on his bible. "My poor, sweet little baby." She kissed the crown of his head and nuzzled into his neck. He could feel the wetness of her tears as her eyes welled. He didn't bother trying to stop his own from tearing up as he sat limply in her embrace. "You've been so misled by the enemy," she whispered sadly.

He forced out a weak, weary, "Mom?"

"Of course God doesn't make mistakes, Sweetheart." She hugged him even tighter to her, and he grunted. She released him so she could pull back and look him the eye. Frowning at the look of devastated resignation on his face, she reached up and carefully wiped his tears away. Unable to hold her gaze for even a nanosecond, Devon let his eyes fall shut and slumped forward. She caught him, hugging him tight again, and he tried to focus on the warmth of her body and the sound of her heart beating in her chest, to keep from falling to pieces. As she spoke again, her tone grew firm and resolute. "You're forgetting something so important, my sweet girl. The Devil is a deceiver, and his favourite pastime is corrupting God's beautiful creations." She sighed heavily and began to rock Devon as if he were still her helpless baby. "God gave me a glorious daughter, and The Deceiver came along to warp her precious mind."

Devon took in a few, shaky breaths and mumbled against her chest pitifully. "But Mom, don't you love me?"

She gently guided him to sit up, and cradled his chin in her hands, waiting silently until he opened his eyes. He refused to look at her, keeping his eyes averted out of self-preservation. Sighing, she wiped away his fresh tears and spoke softly. "I love you more than anything, Devon. We both do, your father and I. Unconditionally. Do you really feel unloved, Baby Girl?"

Devon sniffled and wearily turned his head away, to stare at the blurred colors flashing across the TV screen. He ignored the gentle touch of his mother's finger's tracing the side of his face. *I don't know Mom.* He rubbed his chest, between his developing breasts, trying to soothe out an ache that sat heavy in his soul. *Is this really supposed to make me feel loved right now?* Knowing better than to voice his thoughts, he continued to stare blankly at the TV.

When his mother wrapped him up in her arms again, he allowed it, falling against her like a ragdoll. He ignored her as she rubbed his back and squeezed his shoulder in her attempts to soothe him. He heard her voice and felt the vibrations of her speech against his ear. He knew she was praying now, but he didn't understand the words, nor did he care to. He kept watching the bright colors dance as his heart finally gave up and broke beyond repair.

The empty room reeked of sterility, as if his mother had gone overboard with the bleach, and the whiteness of the walls was so intense Devon had to shut his eyes against it. The air shifted and crept around him, slowly taking on an inescapable weight. The intangible mass bore down on his shoulders—forced him down onto his knees, then his hands, and finally flat on his stomach against the bare, chilled floor. Still, the weight eased down on him, overloading his neurons with messages of agony, stealing the air from his lungs, and slowly squeezing the life out of his heart. It was at the exact point that Devon could sense Death reaching for him, just shy of wrapping bony fingers around his ankle, that the weight stopped. That isn't to say that it vanished. It merely paused, making sure Devon understood how easily he could be crushed.

A booming voice crashed against his ear drums, nearly shattering them. Devon wished he could scream.

"You're corrupted."

The voice was eerie—somehow an exact mimicry of both his mother and his father at the same time but with an Old Testament force and wrath behind it. "Such rotted flesh does not come from me."

The weight on his body did not disappear, but the ground did, and there was a roiling rush in Devon's gut that made him want to vomit as he began to drop.

"Fall from my sight," commanded the voice.

The wind whipped so fiercely against him as he fell, he was unable to close his eyes or mouth. His eyeballs, dry and stinging, seemed to slam back against his brain, and bones began breaking from the speed of his descent.

His mouth hung wide open, in a silent scream, as he blinked his eyes open to reality. He found himself laying on his stomach, on the floor, tangled up in his bedsheets. His head was throbbing slightly.

"I fell out of bed," he panted. His jackrabbit pulse thrummed in his temples, and he took a moment try and calm it by slowing down his breathing. After a series of deep, full breaths, he finally righted himself. As he moved to climb back into bed, he noticed the thick, slick warmth starting to soak the front of his underwear and grimaced. "Oh God," he croaked. "I'm not ready." His next breath, harsh and short, ended in a whimper, and the next one grew even shorter as

I'm not ready, God started spinning in his head. He gripped the edge of his bed, sucked in as deep a breath as his lungs could hold, and counted to four before releasing it again. "Don't panic," he soothed himself. "You knew this was coming." He bit back an urge to cry and curse, and pushed himself back off the bed, trying to fortify himself by standing tall and straight-backed. "Don't panic, you've only got yourself here." His mother had done only the bare minimum to prepare him, preaching, "Once you start your period, you become a woman, with a woman's sacred gift and a woman's responsibilities." She'd explained how to put on panty liners and pads before emphasizing in her steeliest tones, "Using a tampon is an affront to God and your future husband." After that, she had been decidedly tight-lipped, other than to repeat what little she'd already offered. Devon took that to mean he would be on his own, whenever it finally happened, and so he had no room to fall apart now. Holding himself like one of his mother's delicate glass animals, he hobbled over to his dresser, fished out a fresh pair of underwear and hobbled down the hall to the bathroom, where his mother had preemptively stashed a box of menstrual pads as if hiding a dark, dirty secret.

Devon's period had hit fast, and hard. Only four days in, he was already wholly convinced that periods were The Devil's true work and in his most miserable, pain-ridden moments, he wondered if he'd make it out alive. His father had never seemed more uncomfortable around him and miraculously found all manner of handyman jobs around the house to keep himself scarce during the evenings. Even his mother had been taken by surprise, putting aside her own embarrassment to see to Devon's comfort as much as possible.

"You poor thing," she sighed as she breezed into his room. She pulled the covers off Devon and carefully adjusted a freshly filled hot water bottle on his abdomen. "None of the McGinty women have ever had such heavy periods. Especially not for their first cycle. This must come from your father's side."

"Thanks, Mom." He groaned as she fixed the covers and fussed over him. He tried to smile at her but only managed a pained grimace. "You sure it's okay for me to miss Church this week?"

She fixed him with a stern look. "Don't be ridiculous, Sweetheart. You're not going anywhere." She kissed him softly on the cheek and immediately wiped the lipstick stain off his skin. "Please rest. Don't forget to drink lots of water." Her face briefly flushed, and she went about straightening her pearls and her dress. "And check your pad regularly," she half-whispered. "We don't want to ruin your sheets." She turned and left, stopping at his door to say, "I love you, Sweetheart."

Devon mumbled an acknowledgment and closed his eyes. He curled his hands over the top of the hot water bottle, listened to the sounds of departure and was asleep before he knew it.

Devon's gangling body stretched out in a casual, innocuous parody of the Cross as he floated upon the perfectly warm, placid water. He could feel the joy radiate from his core and exude out through his very pores with each rise and fall of his flat chest and each tickle of water against his bare scrotum. "This must be what Adam felt like," he mused aloud in sleepy contentment, "before The Fall." He made the smallest movement with his arms, setting himself spinning in a slow, ambling circle as he laughed. "Or maybe this is what it's like in the womb." As if summoned, the steady lub-dub, lub-dub, lub-dub of a resting heartbeat broke the serene silence, reverberating in his ears and making the water ripple around him. He chuckled and opened his eyes. His pupils expanded, shrunk, and expanded again, trying to catch some light, but there was only the vast inky darkness.

"Yeah, this must be like the womb." He rolled into breaststroke position, content to swim and float through these waters forever, but his body refused to follow the commands his brain had given. He rolled onto his side instead, his face submerging halfway. He gasped in alarm, only to have his mouth flooded with sweet and salty water. He quickly gagged the water down and clamped his mouth shut. As much as he tried to extend his muscles and straighten out, his back curled, and his limbs tucked. The lub-dub lub-dub lub-dub boomed louder, beat faster, became frantic as Devon struggled to keep his head above water and stop himself from balling up. His mind whirled, yowling

what's happening, what's happening whatshappeningwhashappning?!

Unable to stop himself, he opened his mouth to scream and choked on another mouthful of water. It felt thicker somehow, and now had the slightest bitterness to it alongside the sweet and sour. As his brain flailed and his muscles screamed in protest, a film began to form over his mouth.

Godwhashappningtome? God! Please!

The roaring, double time rhythm of lub-dub, lub-dub had the waters sloshing violently, throwing Devon back and forth as the film solidified into a thick, slick membrane that shrunk with each desperate, open-mouthed inhale. It clung to his face tighter than skin—pressing painfully against his aching eyeballs and sealing his nostrils shut. The searing sting of broiled needles stabbing deep into his nasal cavities momentarily distracted him until he finally registered the sudden disappearance of whatever membrane had been strangling him. His didn't have any time to catch his breath, however, before a thick, coppery warmth flooded his mouth. *Blood,* his mind supplied. *I'm drow—*

Devon's own strangled shout yanked him roughly from his nightmare, but consciousness offered no relief as Devon's brain tried to process the burning pain that seemed to split his pelvis in two. He whimpered, terrified, when he registered the minerally reek of blood that permeated the air and the slickness that covered his legs and made his stained nightgown sit heavily against his body. He retched violently, unable to keep the bile down. The heaves thankfully came to a quick stop, leaving him shuddering in revulsion and wiping the dribble of spit from his mouth with the sleeve of his pajamas. "Don't think about it," he ordered himself as he gingerly reached down and hiked up his night gown. "Don't think about it." As stubborn as he tried to be, he couldn't stop himself from retching once more as he grabbed the sides of his drenched panties and shoved them down. This time, he was able to keep from vomiting, but only with a herculean effort. An anguished sob and some hot, bitter tears escaped when the hideous mass of bloated pad and ruined underwear hit the floor with a sickeningly heavy plop.

"What's happening to me, God?" He sniveled and wiped his wet eyes with his other sleeve. "Wha—" He sucked in a gasping breath, bearing down on his lip with his teeth and clutching his abdomen as a body-splitting cramp tore through him. Forgetting the state of himself, Devon pressed his forehead up against his closed knees, smearing blood across his face and dampening his hair. Too pained to care, he rolled onto his side and bit his tongue to harness his focus. "I gotta—" Gasping, he stretched his body out and balled it up again, writhing on the soiled bed in an attempt to ease his discomfort.

I really gotta... gotta... poo? Why I gotta poo so bad? His tears were blinding now, making his eyes burn as they mingled with blood and leaving a salty, coppery taste at the corners of his mouth while he fought his bewildering urge. "Have to," he grunted. *Already a disgusting mess*, he reasoned. *Already destroyed bed.* The urge abruptly seized his entire core like a closed clamp, eliciting a startled, agonized yelp and Devon stopped caring. Clenching his jaw, he bore down and pushed. A forceful gasp pulled his mouth open, and his bloodshot, stinging eyes bulged slightly in their sockets as something seemed to grip him right at the core of his heart and rip. A rush of blood, fluid, and matter came bursting from between his thighs and the world went briefly dark.

The pungent smell of blood in various states of dryness, with a hint of feces, brought Devon back to consciousness. She blinked her eyes open and immediately slammed them shut again. She groped around until she felt something dry and pulled it towards her, to wipe off her face. Blinking her eyes open a second time, she sat up straight and assessed the scene. Her bedsheets were destroyed with all manner of bodily excretions, probably her mattress as well. Peering over the side of her bed, she noted the damp, dark pile leaking blood down into the carpet. She looked down at herself as well and saw nothing but blood-soaked cloth and blood-smeared skin. She pulled her dirty fingers through her hair, trying to untangle the spots that were beginning to matt. That was when she finally caught sight of the kiwi-sized lump of translucent meat. Dispassionately, her gaze followed the bluish-white cord that connected the strange matter to another lump of meat, this one dark like a bruise. It looked just like the posters Dr. Lee had up in his exam room—the ones that her mother always tried to divert her attention from with a bright pink face. "Oh," she said simply as she scooted close and picked up the fetus. Her inspection was cut short when the door flew open.

"Devon? We thought we hear—" Lindy cut herself off with a shrill screech and threw herself into Paul's arms.

Paul stumbled back, but braced himself before they could tumble over. His body heaved at the sight before them, but he kept the bile at bay, forcibly swallowing it back down with a shudder and a disgusted groan. He couldn't tell if the tightness in his chest came from his mounting anxiety, or the clawing hold Lindy had on him. His back stung from the sharp press of her nails through his night shirt, and his chest slickened with the wetness of her tears, saliva and snot soaking through the fabric on the front side. He could feel the frenzy of her words and sobs against him, but all he heard was the adrenaline-crazed pounding of his own heartbeat and the heavy huffs of his own exhales as he breathed though his open mouth. *Lord,* he closed his eyes and tried to steady his breathing, *give me the strength to act.*

He opened his eyes the same moment he finally snapped his mouth shut and gave Lindy a reassuring hug and a kiss atop her head before gently prying her arms off and stepping forward, towards the bed. He retched again at the rich, mineral scent of the room and the horrendous gore covering his daughter's bed. He slapped a hand over his mouth, to keep from vomiting, and waited for the nausea to subside.

There was an unsure, weak squeeze of his shoulder and Lindy's voice sounded next to him—rough, worn, and wavering. "Baby Girl? You—You were pregnant?"

Devon dropped the fetus carelessly and cocked her head, studying her parents curiously. "Of course not, Mother." The flat tone and formality planted seeds of dread deep down in Paul's gut. "A virgin could never be with

77

child." An almost robotic imitation of a smile crudely unfurled across her face, making Paul back up, bumping into Lindy.

Remember your role, he chastised himself as he gently tugged her forward and enveloped her in a secure, fortifying embrace. He was unsure which one of them he was truly trying to soothe. He cleared his throat and threw his voice with as much authority as he could muster. "Then what is that?" Unwilling to let go of his wife, he nodded towards the lump of flesh on the bed.

Devon's face relaxed, her body language losing its inhuman stiffness. A sharp smugness replaced it. "This child?" She picked it up by the sickly-looking umbilical cord, letting it dangle grotesquely and eliciting a harsh, gasping wail from Lindy as she cowered back against Paul's front. Paul wanted to jump forward and rip the fetus from Devon's hands before giving her a sound backhanded smack across the mouth. *This isn't my little angel*, he insisted as he tightened his arms around Lindy.

"This," Devon dropped it again with a derisive snort, "is the Devon God had given you." She paused to stare boldly into first her father's eyes, then her mother's. They both shrank back from her glare with matching gasps. "You didn't want him," Devon continued sweetly. "You prayed for him to be replaced with a daughter.

And now, *I* have given that to you." A saccharine smile spread across her face, staying for only a moment before it morphed into a haughty sneer. "Shouldn't you be grateful," she demanded in gruff, deep voice no teenaged girl should be capable of.

Paul felt Lindy shifting in his arms and looked down to her flushed, tear-streaked face. The sting of his own tears made him blink as he watched fear and shame overtake her. "We—We prayed for *this*," she whisper-hissed in disbelief.

"No," he whispered back. He moved a hand up to move the plastered hairs off her face and ran his finger down along the side of her face. He shook his head sadly before throwing his attention back to their daughter. "No," he practically screamed, his voice pitched unnaturally high. He let go of Lindy and stepped forward, throwing his hands accusingly at Devon as she moved to perch on the edge of her bed and waited. "This isn't what we prayed for at all," he seethed.

Devon let out a hair-raising laugh that froze him in place. He dropped his hands down to his sides and stared at her, slack-jawed once again.

Devon shook her head and tsk'ed playfully. "What is prayer but an outgoing call?" She hopped down off her bed and moved towards him. Paul blanched and gagged at the sight of his daughter's ruined nightgown sticking to her blood-slick thighs and the crimson rivulets trickling down her legs to stain the carpet as she swayed past him. Mesmerized in his disgust, he could only turn and watch Devon's progress across the room.

"God isn't the only one who can answer a call," she pointed out in a sing-song voice as she came to a stop inches from her mother. Lindy whimpered and trembled, but stood her ground, unable to run and hide from her own daughter. She clasped and unclasped her hands, her facial muscles twitching nervously as she forced herself to hold Devon's gaze. Smirking, Devon reached up with a bloodied hand and caressed her face, leaving wet red trails on her cheek that made Lindy tremble harder. "And just as you had told your son; I do so love corrupting what He has made."

PERFECT TEETH

The chitter chatter of teeth knocking together, as if someone were freezing, pulls him back into consciousness. He opens his eyes, yawns, and goes to stretch.

Panic seizes his mind as his body firmly refuses to move. All he can do is blink frantically and snap his mouth shut and open again, like a fish. He can feel his vocal cords tremble, but the silence remains undisturbed.

Well, except for those chattering teeth.

Only now does he register the crushing weight bearing down on his chest, and he pushes the pain in and out with short, labored breaths. Tears well at the corners of his eyes as his helpless gaze focuses on the barely discernible figure hunched atop his sternum.

Those teeth are all he can truly see. They abruptly stop knocking together and settle into an unnaturally broad grin. The whitest, most eerily straight and perfectly aligned set of teeth he has ever seen, with the sharpest canines. He imagines just the smallest graze would be like running the corner of a fresh razor blade along his flesh, pictures the seams of his cut skin easing apart like room temperature butter.

That unnerving smile moves closer, eliciting a silent gasp and the desire to recoil. Now he can make out what he supposes must be eyes, deep recesses just above the grin with tiny pinpoints of blazing scarlet at the centers.

The scream that he can't let out builds in the depths of his diaphragm, roaring and echoing inside his head. The jackrabbit pulse of his frenzied heart would make him wince in pain, were he not petrified into forcing his eyes to remain fawn wide. His palms are sickeningly cool with the sheen of sweat as he frantically tries to move even just a single finger. The agony in his chest has become unbearable, and he begins to hyperventilate.

Unable to withstand the strain, he slams his eyes shut, causing warm, salty tears to trail down toward his ears. Just as the prick of those canines slices him open . . .

A cool breath tickles his ear, followed by an unintelligible whisper that bounces off his eardrum. It reverberates in his mind, planting a seed of dread and doom. He's grateful that he's unable to make out the message.

Crying, he begs God for a deep, dreamless sleep.

Late morning sunlight has made his room pleasantly warm, and he cracks his eyes open, feeling as though he's been hit by a pillowcase full of bricks. All the same, he forces himself out of bed and through his morning routine. He mustn't be late to his afternoon appointment. He's eager to tell his therapist the nightmares have started again.

Soon enough, though still not quite soon enough to suit him, he finds himself in his usual spot on the couch. He tries not to tap his feet, or fold his arms across his chest, or otherwise fidget as the other man straightens some papers on his desk and fusses over his potted plant. Finally, Dupont grabs his notepad and pen and comes around his desk, to sit closer.

Dupont makes himself comfortable in his usual leather chair, readies his pen, and throws his gaze over to his patient. He offers a wide smile. His pearly white teeth have to be the straightest, most perfectly aligned set in existence, and his canines look about ready to rip through a thick, juicy cut of steak.

A scream rips itself from the deepest depths of his diaphragm, booming in the late-night still of his bedroom like thunder as he shoots up in bed. His eyes fly open and he clutches wildly at his chest. Minutes crawl by while he slowly comes to trust reality. His pulse has calmed, but his muscles still throb with tension as he focuses on the flashing red numbers of his alarm clock that tell him only about twenty minutes have passed since he gave in to sleep.

Unease spills down his spine like frigid water.

BELIEVE ME NOW?

Everything was new.

To Claire, it felt like they'd barely had time to unpack from their honeymoon before it was time for Justin to move on to the next duty station. They had planned it that way, of course—the sooner the wedding happened, the sooner she could be entered into the system as a dependent, and best for it to be done before the next Permanent Change of Station—but the breakneck speed of it all left her a bit winded. A new duty station for Justin meant a new state for Claire, and while she understood it was just as new for him, she couldn't stop thinking, *He moved away from home years ago. He's already used to this.*

At least there was something positive about all this change: their first house. As cookie-cutter as it was, as annoying as it may prove to be that they shared a wall with the next-door neighbor, it was the first house Claire had ever been in after a lifetime spent in apartments. Having a house to turn into a home with her brand-new husband went a long way in taming the homesickness that sometimes tried to rear its head as unearned resentment. That is, until she first noticed the scratching. An intermittent *scritch scratch* over their heads as they snuggled on the couch to enjoy the prime-time lineup. *Isn't this how it always starts?* Claire asked herself sullenly. From the first apartment they'd shared, she already knew not to bother pointing it out to Justin. When the all-too-familiar dread lodged itself at the base of her spine, she kept quiet and busied herself with putting the house in order and deciding how she should decorate.

One Tuesday night, when the scratching was especially hard to ignore, Justin surprised her by gently nudging her off his side and pushing up from the couch with a heavy sigh. "Enough's enough. Better check this out."

Claire gaped at him, dumbfounded. "You hear it too?" She got up and followed him to the garage.

"Of course I do." He stepped back into the house with the stepladder, a flashlight, and an amused smile. "Get the door for me?"

Claire tried not to give an excited clap or giggle as she pulled the garage door shut and turned to walk over into the hall. For the first time in her life, after all the places she'd lived that set her nerves on edge, someone else noticed too. *Maybe I can tell him after all. He's got to believe me now*, she reasoned with no small satisfaction as he went up the ladder and disappeared into the crawl space that Housing called an attic.

"It's clean as a whistle," he reported upon coming back down and putting things away. "No signs of critters."

"But you hear it," she insisted, doing her best not to come across as a nag.

"Yeah, it's weird, alright." He shrugged and leaned in to kiss her cheek. "But I'm telling you, there's nothing there."

As they stood still, watching each other, there came a sudden, single *scritch* right above his head, drawing his gaze up to the ceiling; and she was certain he would come to what she considered the only logical conclusion.

"Mice maybe," he muttered as he looked back at her.

Realizing she'd been hoping for the impossible, she sagged in defeat.

"Must've missed them," he concluded.

That proved to be his final say on the matter, but not anything close to an end. No matter how many times he went back up to investigate, there was nothing to see. No matter how many traps he set, the scratching never stopped; and since neither search nor trap could yield results, he felt it was a waste of time to call Maintenance. Many times, she pointed out to him that the scratching was only ever above their heads, and not even once did it spread out through the rest of the house.

"Don't you find that strange?" she asked him with increasing petulance.

The only answer he had for her was an increasingly tight smile, with an increasingly impatient look in his eye. "It's not that big a deal, is it?" He always softened his argument with a gentle, reassuring squeeze of her shoulder that only ever made her bite the inside of her lip to stay composed. "We don't find droppings anywhere, we don't see anything running around, nothing gets into the food. Why bother? It's not even a constant thing. Just a little scratching here and there."

She stopped talking about the house after that, stopped bothering to go to him for comfort when she woke up multiple times a night. She did her best to grin and bear it all the times she felt the air gather around her and take on a weight that perched on her shoulders. When she began to feel invisible fingers tangle in her hair and hear faraway, hissing whispers, she stayed silent and smiled at him more sweetly than ever. She took up gardening to stay outside as long as she could. He praised her, clearly buying her act and thinking her admirably house-proud. When she began avoiding the rest of the house, sticking to the front room that looked out onto the front walk and was too small to be anything other than a cozy reading nook, he only grinned and gave her kisses. "My little bookworm," he called her.

One suspiciously calm Friday found Claire stretched out in bed, soaking up the warmth of the bright afternoon sunlight that filtered in through the open venetian blinds as she flipped through the latest issue of *Better Homes & Gardens*.

She was on the verge of a smile and a lazy, contented hum when her mind seemed to snap to attention and her body automatically stiffened, her fingers crumpling the paper as her hands tensed into fists. Before her brain could fully form the command, she was tilting her head back to look up at the ceiling. She only just barely spotted the large black shadow before it hurtled across the ceiling and somehow completely out of sight. The immediate fear had her frozen in place as she listened to her thundering heartbeat and told herself, *Just keep breathing*.

Instead of telling Justin about the inexplicable shadow when he came home, she smiled and suggested they go to the pound and adopt a dog.

"I thought you didn't like dogs," he pointed out, trying to keep his excitement in check.

"I just never had one, that's all." It was true, she had never had a dog, but that was irrelevant. She was desperate to feel safe.

The dog, a Labrador named Blondie, seemed just as anxious about the house as she was. All the same, she did feel a bit better—at least she wasn't alone in knowing the house was wrong somehow.

Claire worked hard at maintaining the facade that, as far as Justin knew, their life was falling into place. Her con was successful, and she felt gratified by his oblivious happiness. His contentment even trickled down to her. *After all, I have always wanted to be somebody's wife*, she reflected when he showered her with his easy, everyday affection. Her happiness, though, only went as far as that unshakable unease allowed. She tried to calm it by talking to her doctor, getting him to adjust her prescriptions. She tried to mitigate it by attempting small talk with the neighbors at every opportunity, going out on long walks with Blondie during the day, and sometimes, taking evening strolls with Justin. At the end of the day, though—every day—she was still stuck in the house.

Then, he went away. The first deployment cycle since they'd gotten together, and the house seemed to spring to life, as if it had been waiting for the skeptic to get out of its way.

Only a couple weeks in, Claire had already assembled an arsenal of mantras to help her get through each day. *It's such a cute house*, she reminded herself whenever she got out of her car and started up the front walk. Whenever she tended to her various planters, she whispered to the flowers, "I've always wanted a backyard, and now, I finally have one." Every Monday, as she moved about the house with her duster, she tried to rekindle some of the joy she'd felt on their walk-through of the unit. *It's so nice to have a guest room*, she replayed those words in her head as she got up on the stepladder to reach the top of the fan blades. *And it'll be the perfect nursery someday.* Every day, as she led Blondie out the front door to go for a walk, she'd tell them how nice the weather always seemed to be in San Diego.

An affirmation for every possible circumstance, and yet, they never seemed to have a lasting effect. All the good they might've done would be immediately obliterated just as soon as Claire heard another series of scratches from inside the walls or felt invisible eyes observing her from the hallway as she tried to read in her little front room sanctuary.

The darting shadow, which she had been utterly thankful not to have seen after that first sighting, now teased her peripheral vision just often enough to keep her growing paranoia well fed. Blondie seemed to stay in the house only out of a sense of duty. They would yip and bark happily and wag their tail and dart out in front of her any time she opened the glass sliding door to go tend to her flower-box garden. They would sit by the front door, leash between their teeth, whimpering, until she was ready to go out for their walks. Inside the house, Blondie followed her solemnly, never leaving her side unless she went into the bathroom. No matter how she cajoled and pleaded, or even shouted and threatened, Blondie would never go in there, and it took bribery to get Blondie into the primary bedroom every night.

Seeing no other solution, she eventually brought in a priest to bless the house. She'd never been one to subscribe to religion herself, but desperate times called for desperate measures. Having nothing to go on except popular culture, she had hoped to get a Catholic in, as that seemed the most proper choice, but found them wholly unwilling to humor her since she wasn't a Catholic herself. She settled for the pastor at the nearby Presbyterian church, Pastor Thomas.

He came by on a Wednesday afternoon.

"Is there any particular room you'd like to start in?" he asked after the expected pleasantries and small talk.

She smiled and led him to the bathroom. "I can't stand being in here, especially at night." She reached around the doorjamb and turned on the light before she passed the threshold and stood awkwardly with her back to the medicine cabinet's mirrored door. "It just feels too much like I'm being watched. It's so creepy." She gestured past the priest to Blondie, who sat just outside the doorway, body tense and big, soft eyes silently pleading with her to come back out. "She won't even come in at all."

Just as Claire was opening her mouth to continue, Pastor Thomas abruptly reached over and flipped the light switch.

Claire let out a short shriek as she stumbled backward, catching herself on the sink, and Blondie snapped to her defensive stance, barking in alarm.

Pastor Thomas turned the light back on, a look of concern forming on his face. Claire could've sworn she'd seen a flicker of a smirk just before, but was too stunned to really let the suspicion sink in. "Are you okay?" he asked in a convincingly concerned tone.

"You—you turned off the light," she stammered. "Why would you do that?"

Even he seemed confused as he stopped to consider the question. "I'm not sure," he admitted. "To see what you would do?"

Blondie stood in the hall anxiously, her teeth bared as she growled at him.

"I'm— I need you to leave," Claire spat at him. "Get out now!"

Not needing to be told twice, he carefully edged past Blondie and beat a hasty retreat.

Claire waited until she heard the front door shut behind him and then the sound of his engine turning over before she moved, launching herself out of the bathroom and not bothering to turn out the light. "Let's go out back," she blurted to Blondie.

Every day was the same, with scratches spreading all throughout the walls and ceilings and floorboards, and shadows encroaching farther and farther into her line of vision, until she didn't even try to find excuses to leave the house anymore. It all seemed so pointless if she would always have to return afterward.

"Everyone here is so fake," she spat out on one of her increasingly rare phone calls home. She tugged the quilt up and wrapped it around her shoulders before silently coaxing Blondie up onto the bed. "I thought I'd made some friends." A bitter laugh burst out of her before she could continue, and Blondie gave a concerned huff before nestling into her side. "As if that hadn't been hard enough to begin with, making friends here. It's like some club, only moms allowed. You gotta breed to be worth knowing or to be worth anyone's support." She could hear her sister's intake of breath as she got ready to reply and quickly cut her off. "Know how long it took the bitch right across from us to walk over and introduce herself? Months, Jackie. It took months before she would do more than just wave at me, and then she comes in with her 'We gotta look out for each other, I'm always here for you' bullshit."

"Well," Jackie said in her most careful devil's-advocate tone, "was her husband—"

"No, Jackie. No, her husband's on shore duty. He's been here all along. He is here. He's not going anywhere. He doesn't work weird hours. She just decided I wasn't worth welcoming right away. And you know what? Mrs. We're-A-Community hasn't been back since, and anytime I've tried going over to her, she's always way too busy. And don't even get me started on the people next door. I can hear them through the wall sometimes and see them getting in and out of their car, but they might as well be imaginary for all the times we've interacted. Imagine *sharing a wall* with somebody and not even knowing their name! And you know the friends I thought I had? Lisa and Kelly?"

"Yeah, Claire. I remember you mentioning them."

"You shoulda seen how quick they went to pretending I don't exist once I stopped going out to do things all the time. It's all just such a lie. No one, Jackie. No one is making any effort to check in with me or ask if I'm okay or—"

"Sis?"

Claire stopped to take a breath. She was only *sis* when Jackie was especially worried or feeling vulnerable herself. "Yeah?" She tried calming herself by giving Blondie long, slow pets from the top of their head down to the base of their tail. Blondie huffed softly in approval.

"Why don't you just come home? That's something a lot of wives do, isn't it? Go back home during deployment? It's not like you guys have any kids yet. Please, just come home."

There was a long pause as Claire took several deep breaths, in through her nose and out through her mouth as she counted. It did little to keep the tears at bay, but it did help her keep her voice even as she replied, "That's not really something I can do right now, Jacks. You know that already. And yeah, we don't have kids yet, but there's Blondie. I'm sorry, but I just have to stay put. Remember, Jacks, no need to stress Mom out. As far as she knows, everything's great, alright?"

Before Jackie could give any kind of response, Claire faked an excited squeal that made Blondie give a half-hearted bark. "Oh, oh my God! Jacks, I gotta go. Justin is texting me! They must've reached a port! Love you, gotta go." She practically stabbed the red phone icon in her haste and let out a long, heavy sigh.

"So much for getting each other through this life," she muttered to Blondie as she gently scratched the dog's ruff.

The days continued to drift by in a slow, anxious haze. If Claire wasn't in her reading chair, she was out back sending emails to her husband and posting beautiful white lies on social media. Soon enough, she stopped doing even that. It was just her and Blondie trapped in the house, waiting for an email, or a message, or a phone call from Justin, waiting for him to come home.

Then, one night she woke up because Blondie was growling.

They're having a doggie nightmare, she told herself. She closed her eyes to go back to sleep, but Blondie would not stop growling, and her skin started to crawl with goose bumps. She sat up in bed and reached out to click on the bedside lamp. When she saw the dog, she let out a gasp and clutched at her own throat. Blondie was sitting straight up and staring at the bed, right at the empty spot where Justin would be if he were home. Blondie glared and growled, their lips curling up over their teeth and their whole body tense.

When she turned to see who was in bed with her, there was no one there, but she could feel someone meeting her gaze dead-on.

With a little shriek that died in her throat almost as soon as it started, she leaped out of bed, rushed to the door, and flung it open. Blondie followed her out into the hall, and they ran straight to that little front room, her safe zone. Blondie noticed first and stopped to cower behind her, whimpering.

Someone was already there, sitting in her chair.

Someone that looked exactly like her, except they didn't look afraid. They looked like they were having the time of their life.

"Who are you?" she tried to scream, but the question came out choked by her sobbing.

"Isn't it obvious?" they asked in her own voice.

"You're not me!" She pointed a trembling finger. "You—you're the house! You're trying to—to—"

"To what? You're doing this to yourself." Standing, they put down the book they'd been reading, then stepped forward.

"No!" She took a step backward, nearly tripping over Blondie who let out a startled yelp. "Stay away from me."

This made them stop, but they only popped their hip defiantly and crossed their arms over their chest, tapping their fingertips against their elbows. "Now how am I supposed to do that?" they teased. "I'm you and you're me. We're all we have, hun."

Claire kept retreating until she found herself pressed up against the wall. Blondie cowered in front of her, trying to growl menacingly, even as she pressed back into Claire and shook.

"We've got to get each other through this life." They mimicked the woman across the street precisely, right down to the exact pitch and inflection, with sadistic glee written all over their face.

Claire closed her eyes against the well of tears that had collected at the inner corners and tried to pick out the sound of her breathing over the thundering *thump*, *thump*, *thump* of her pulse. Her hands moved mechanically, trying to soothe Blondie with gentle pets and hugs. Blondie whimpered and tensed in her arms, their body going still even though Claire could feel their heart race just as fast as her own.

She blinked her eyes open and couldn't hold back a scream. It lurched out past her lips, moving the hair that fell in front of the other Claire's face and leaving spittle on the other Claire's cheek. They took up the last remaining bit of space, touching the tip of their nose to hers, and whispered, "The fun is just beginning."

As her body double continued to step forward, forcing her harder and harder up against the wall until she found herself disappearing into it, Claire let out one more earsplitting scream that could be heard clearly in the stillness of the evening.

More than one of her neighbors took note, but none of them called the police—military or otherwise—not over one solitary scream. Blondie's frantic, relentless barking, however, quickly led to a noise complaint that brought the MPs straight to the house. As far as they were concerned, once they got Management to let them in with the master key, Claire was nowhere to be found.

She had no idea what her plan was, if she managed to get herself noticed, but Claire ran her fingernails against the inside of the walls all the same. Blondie whimpered sadly, trying to alert the woman petting them to Claire's presence, but the officer only tried to shush them soothingly and threw out a command to her partner. "Hey, check the garage for a leash."

"Let's see if one of the neighbors can take the dog," he tossed over his shoulder as he moved toward the garage door. "I wanna hurry up and get outta here. Either this place is full of mice or there's some demon shit going on." He laughed half-heartedly. "This place is bad vibes."

Only minutes later, the MPs—with a reluctant, whimpering Blondie in tow—were headed across the street to talk with the neighbor that had made the call.

The walls seemed to sigh with Claire as she watched them go. She wondered how long she would be alone before the Red Cross got an emergency message out to Justin's ship and his command sent him home.

Well, she thought as she stretched herself all throughout the house, *at least there's no way he won't believe me now*. A prick of amusement caught her by surprise, and she realized the house hadn't exactly been lying to her when it had told her the fun was just beginning. *I'll show him exactly how wrong this place is.*

BIRTHDAY SUIT

They'd come across the cassette tape during a walk through the woods. It was an ordinary Memorex HBII, the label left blank, and the badly cracked case missing its J-card. They'd made some of their favorite music discoveries thanks to garage sale buys and abandoned cassettes, so they had been only too eager to pocket it and take it home. Now they stood in their bedroom, a palpable excitement thickening the air as they waited to hear their latest find.

It started so low—barely perceptible—but the baritone pulse strengthened within seconds, emboldened by a rolling cymbal rain. It left them taut and poised, shards of anticipation under their skin, until the punch of drum snapped them into action.

They seemed out of their own body—out of their own control—as they moved to the cut of the serrated riffs and the insistent, pounding beat, that baritone thrum always in the background. Images flashed through their mind, colorless and gritty, like an arthouse film: dancing bare feet, fluid limbs, and sweat-slick hair flicking to and fro as heads tilted back and offered oblivious expressions up to the sky.

Entranced by the sound reverberating through them and their own impulsive movements, they felt at one with the cavorting crowd—part of a mysterious ritual. They could feel something rising. Some unknown, primordial sense, dark and menacing only because of its foreignness. The dance continued, the strange instinct grew and overtook, until he could feel the exhilaration surging through his veins.

He felt good, felt himself.

Eventually, the sawing guitar buzzed into feedback, which faded into nothing, and he stopped as if someone had flipped a switch. He felt pleasantly wrung out as he strode over to his bedroom door. He had to see his flushed, joyous features for himself.

Colleen grinned at her reflection. The confusion and insatiable need to self-analyze had yet to creep in and settle. For now, she only felt good and right in the universe.

The new transfer at school had to be an illusion. There was no other way to explain their ephemeral nature. Their features seemed to shift with the light, flickering in and out—*male, female, androgynous,* and so on. Looking at them, Colleen never could pin down one specific impression. Even stranger still, they seemed to blend in seamlessly, no matter where she spotted them, and to have no effect on their surroundings nor to be affected by them themself. It occurred to Colleen eventually that she might be the only one to see them at all. Anytime she asked about them, describing them as best she could, she'd be met with puzzled expressions, apologetic shakes of the head, or needlessly harsh speculations on her sanity.

After maddening weeks, bordering on months, of trying to find this mysterious shifter, Colleen happened upon them when she was least expecting it and in the most mundane place: loitering outside the Circle K she passed on her way home from school. Almost as if they had been waiting for her. Dumbfounded, Colleen came to a sudden halt and stood, blinking, for a long beat before she finally approached. They didn't budge, simply enjoyed a soda and allowed her to make the first move.

Up close, they didn't shift with the light. They were reassuringly solid and present but still failed to give Colleen a definitive sense of anything. They wore one too many layers of too-loose clothing for her to be able to discern a chest, but Colleen knew full well that their breasts might just be small, like her own. Their face still had a touch too much baby fat, with angles just a bit too soft to look male, but perhaps they just hadn't started growing into their pubescent changes. Their hair and makeup, of course, were no help. They could be a girl just as easily as they could be a boy that wanted to look cool, like all the pop stars. *Gender bending* everyone called it. After all, wouldn't Colleen have close-cropped hair just like Annie Lennox if only she could? If only her parents hadn't decreed that she was far too old to be a tomboy, that it was time for her to finally grow up and become a proper young lady? She absently scowled and reached back to pull the scrunchy out of her hair, putting it around her left wrist like a bracelet and reaching back again to fan out and fidget with her cinnamon waves.

"What are you thinking about so deeply over there?" They pushed off the wall and offered a teasing grin. "I'd hate to think that scowl was meant for me."

Colleen blushed and looked away for a moment. "Sorry." She looked back up, sheepish. Her eyes traveled up their body and back down again, slowly, and she chewed on her lower lip in contemplation before finally meeting their gaze. "Can I ask you kind of a rude question?"

The tease was back in their smile as they regarded her silently. Colleen had brushed her hair forward, over one shoulder, and now she finger-combed it anxiously. Goose bumps rose on her skin under their scrutiny.

They finally broke the tension with a mirth-filled chuckle. "There's only one way to find out."

Colleen twisted her hair around her fingers and tugged, to soothe her nerves as she spoke. "Are you a girl or a boy?"

Their smile widened, and their lips parted to show teeth. Their hazel eyes seemed to shine like gold as they leaned in and answered, "Neither." They caught the straw in their mouth and sipped their fountain drink with an affected primness that normally would've made Colleen laugh, if she weren't so stuck on that single word.

Her jaw dropped, and her fingers began to comb and tug faster as she attempted to order and process her thoughts. "Neither?" She shook her head, as if that would help put everything into its proper context. "Is that—" She leaned in now, her face etched with disbelief, but her eyes glinting with hidden hope and excitement. "Can you do that? Be neither?" She frowned when she noticed an older couple throwing the two of them a disapproving look as they walked into the store. Noting her discomfort, the stranger moved a little farther down, toward the small field behind the parking lot. Colleen followed gratefully and waited for the conversation to continue.

Once they were comfortably out of earshot, they stopped and turned back to give a small shrug before speaking in a soft yet authoritative tone. "Identity isn't something other people allow. It's something that just is. I'm not a girl or a boy, I'm just . . ."

The way they had trailed off felt like an invitation, and she accepted without thought. "A person?"

Colleen took their silence and sly expression for her answer.

"I'm Diana, by the way." They smirked, deeply amused.

A fresh blush bloomed furiously across Colleen's cheeks, and she threw her gaze down to the dying grass. "Oh my God, duh. Sorry!" She shook her head at herself and looked up again, with a shy smile. "Colleen."

Diana took another long sip from their straw until there was the telltale *schleerp* of getting down to the last drops of soda. They brought their emptied cup down from their mouth and gave Colleen an unabashedly assessing look. "I've been thinking . . ." They trailed off again, inciting Colleen's curiosity.

"Thinking what?" She fidgeted with the shoulder straps of her backpack as she waited with an open, eager expression.

"You seem like one of us." They gestured to themself with their cup. "Like me, I mean. A kindred spirit."

"I'm not—" Colleen stepped back and shrugged, scuffing her shoe on a bald patch of dirt. "I'm not neither."

"Of course not." Diana closed the distance between them and leaned back in.

Colleen found herself mirroring the movement until their foreheads almost touched, and her hair fell forward like a curtain to keep their conversation private.

"But you're definitely not a girl," Diana whispered, "are you?"

It took Colleen's brain a few minutes to catch up to the conversation. She'd never had someone ask her such a bold question, so plainly. She'd also never met someone who genuinely seemed to care about the answer, not the way she suspected Diana cared. She pulled away, straightening to her full height, then thought better of it and came closer again instead. She brought her mouth as close to Diana's face as possible without whispering in their ear and spoke in a small, secretive tone. "I don't want to be. I feel wrong this way." She rested her hand on Diana's shoulder without thinking and this time did whisper directly into their ear. "Something's not right. It's really wrong, and it's suffocating me." She clamped her teeth down on her lower lip and blinked away a tear.

Diana surprised her by wrapping their arms around her and pulling her in for a hug. It was an awkward embrace, with Diana's arms wrapping around her backpack as well and the cup still clutched in their hand, but it made Colleen feel a sudden surge of comfort and security she never would've expected. It was they who whispered in her ear now. "Are you a boy?"

Colleen nodded and instantly buried her face in the crook of Diana's neck, to hide her embarrassment.

They shifted, moving their free hand to stroke Colleen's hair, as if to say *Shh, it's nothing to be embarrassed about.*

She nuzzled her face in deeper still, her flushed skin hot against them, and wondered how exactly she was having such an intimate conversation with a stranger. *But I've been looking for them so long that they don't feel strange.*

"What's your name?"

The gentle encouragement in their tone warmed Colleen's heart. She pulled back, breaking the embrace, but suddenly felt too scared to look them in the eye. "It's—um." She mechanically went about fixing her hair and worrying at her lower lip. Diana waited patiently, until Colleen finally peered up and answered meekly. "Emery. It's Emery."

"Bitchin'!" Diana nodded as if that made it all official, and Colleen's heart lifted. "So, Emery"— they grinned—"can we hang later?"

Colleen nearly bounced on the balls of her feet and clapped her hands together in her excitement. Befriending Diana seemed like the most important thing in the world at that moment. She tried not to come across too eager and failed spectacularly. "Oh yeah, totally, like, fer sure!"

Diana chuckled fondly and nodded their affirmation. "I'll show you how to be a boy," they threw out with a mysterious, sly look. They were already well on their way back toward the parking lot by the time Colleen had decided she'd heard what she'd heard, and another sharp realization intruded before she could go after them. *How are we going to hang out if we didn't exchange numbers or anything?*

When she looked again, Diana was somehow already gone.

Colleen opened her eyes to find herself curled up in a warm, moist nest of moss. Allowing her mind time to wake up and figure out where she was, she unfurled her body and gave it a good stretch before standing. She took a few minutes to right herself, pulling small twigs and bits of dead leaf out of her hair. Cool, silvery light allowed her a clear view of a large clearing, surrounded by the sharp, pointed silhouettes of pine trees. *Am I back behind the house?* she asked herself, despite knowing she wasn't. She tiptoed forward, inexplicably anxious about disturbing the still, somehow mystical landscape. "Hello?" She turned slowly, trying to catch sight of anything that could ground her. When she had gone full circle, she blinked and had to do a double take. In the center of the clearing sat a table, as large and round as the full moon pinned up in the sky, and around it gathered a small group of people, happily chattering amongst themselves. *How did I not notice that?* She took a few tentative steps forward, her bare feet sinking into the supple ground. Just then, someone turned away from the table, and Colleen's mouth curved into a relieved smile when she saw Diana get up and come toward her. They were dressed in a plain tunic now and sans makeup, but Colleen felt she would've recognized them anywhere.

"Emery, you made it!" They reached her in what seemed like the blink of an eye and pulled her into a tight hug. "Please, come eat with us!" They guided her to the center of the clearing.

Everyone gathered around the table adjusted to face Colleen fully. She looked from blood-smeared face to bloodied smile, the incongruity of the situation forming a fuzzy film of shock over her brain. Having satisfied their curiosity, one of the group brought their attention back to what they'd been doing, drawing Colleen's gaze along with them. "Is that—" Her face wrinkled in disgust as she watched them lovingly finger the bluish-white braid that erupted into thick, protruding veins branching out like tree roots across a large lump of meat in a deep shade of bruised purple. "Is that someone's placenta?" As if to punctuate her question, they leaned in and took a bite out of the umbilical cord, severing it from the rest of the afterbirth. They passed along the placenta, chewing on the end of their umbilical treat as if it were merely a stick of jerky.

Diana softened their face and offered an enticing smile that made their eyes invitingly bright. "You can't create a whole being out of nothing," they pointed out cheerfully. "You must plant a seed."

"This?" Aghast, Colleen eyed the meat on the table one more time. "This is what you meant when you said you'd show me how to be a boy? This is . . . grody." She scrunched up her face and stuck out her tongue.

Diana rested their hand on her shoulder and moved to murmur into her ear. "What I meant, Emery, is that I can make you a boy." They pulled back so they could look her dead in the eye, and she could see the earnestness in their face. "Literally."

"Literally?" The word fell out of Colleen's mouth in a heavy haze of confusion and mistrust.

"Literally," they repeated. "I can help you become Emery. Like, totally for real." They gave her shoulder a squeeze before letting go and straightening to stand to their full height, which somehow seemed a bit taller than just a moment ago. "Don't you want that? You seemed to want it earlier." They shrugged. "Maybe you don't want it enough?"

Panic easily overtook and obliterated all the doubt that had just been gaining traction. She sucked in a deep breath, straightening her spine to stand tall as she did. She held it for a few moments, then let it back out in a sudden rush. "Yeah, I want this." She nodded and took up the last remaining spot at the table. "I really do." She locked gazes with the person to her right and held out her hands, palms up. "I'll eat it."

She had to bite back a groan of distress when they plopped the organ into her hands. It was still warm, and disturbingly mushy. Deep crimson coated her palms as soon as it made contact. She clenched her eyes shut, to get rid of the visual that was making bile rise in her esophagus, and tried to ignore the metallic scent that was so strong she could taste pennies on the back of her tongue. *Just do it, already*, she scolded herself. *One.* She paused, needing to force her muscles to relax. *Two.* She took another centering breath. *Three.*

Keeping her eyes closed, she took a bite. The organ squished between her teeth, giving easily when she used her canines and incisors to tear and pull. Her portion slid onto her tongue in a burst of bitter warmth, the iron-rich blood coating the inside of her cheeks, making them sting. Her mind projected a subtle, sickening *squelch* against her eardrums as her molars ground up the mass of tissue and blood vessels. It slid down her gullet like jelly after only a brief chewing.

She opened her eyes to find herself shivering in the cool night air, huddled into herself on the forest floor. Her nightshirt had bloody fingerprints from where she'd clutched it with sticky hands, and the taste of placenta was still fresh on her tongue.

After that, Colleen only ever saw Diana in dreams—if they were truly dreams—the way she always woke up to find herself lying in the woods back behind her house left her with only questions. She wasn't offered any more organ meat after that first visit to the clearing. Instead, they all danced. Sweat-soaked skin, oblivious minds, and bodies possessed by the insistent beat, the kind of wild, free dancing that always made Emery feel right within himself and within the universe, made him forget all about that girl named Colleen.

Soon enough, Colleen once again woke up in her mossy bed to see the round table in the center of the clearing, the gossamer light of the full moon lending the scene a certain magic. Diana came to meet her with something held carefully in their hands. "Drink this." They thrust a simple earthen cup at her by way of greeting.

She brought it toward her face but paused when a strange odor reached her nose. Just underneath a potent musk, she could detect faint scents of blood and bleach. Her nose wrinkled, pulling the corners of her mouth wide in a tight, skeptical line. "What is this, Diana?"

"Do the details really matter?" Diana offered a sweet expression and gave her shoulder a reassuring squeeze. "Think of it as a vitamin smoothie. Needed nutrients." They patted her belly. "You can't plant a seed and never water it."

Colleen cocked her head, eyeing them dubiously.

Diana chuckled. "You need to trust me." They nodded encouragingly when Colleen brought the cup closer, resting its rim up against the seam of her lips. "Don't worry about what it is, just what it will do for you."

At last, she parted her lips and tilted the cup, gulping down as much as she could in one swallow. The regret was nearly instantaneous, and it took all she had not to throw the cup to the ground and watch it shatter. The revolting combination of mineral-y, sweet, salty, and ever so slightly bitter made her shiver, and she kept herself from throwing it back up by sheer force of will. She coughed, as if that could somehow get the taste out of her mouth, and shoved the cup back toward Diana who took it with gentle patience. "Why was it warm?" Colleen gasped. "And that thickness..." She shivered again. "Kind of like snot. Please tell me I don't need to drink it all!"

"Of course not." Diana rubbed her back soothingly. "You drank enough. It takes some getting used to, I know."

"I don't want to get used to that!" Colleen spat. She met Diana's placid expression with a sneer. "Is this some kind of joke? Totally bogus!"

Diana's face fell for a moment before they pulled it back together into a look of exasperation. "No need to get nasty." Their voice was tight, taking her by surprise and tempering her anger. "This is a process, *girl*."

Colleen cringed. Of all things, having *girl* thrown in her face was the reaction she'd expected least—truthfully, not at all. She bit down hard on her bottom lip to keep herself from pointing out how cruel that was.

Diana took a step closer, seeming to loom over her with a startlingly cold gaze. "You can have what you want, Emery. Be who you should be, but only if you're truly willing. It doesn't seem like you are. Seems like you're the one treating this as a joke. An ancient rite of the liminal. You think you know better than us?"

"Better than us? What does that mean?" The ground seemed to slip away, out from under her feet, while her brain scrambled to process her thoughts and decode the information she had. She finally snapped her mouth shut and regarded Diana with a new sense of trepidation as all the implications she'd been so blithely overlooking fully hit home. "You—you're not human, are you?" she blurted out before they could respond, puzzling out a few more details. "This has all been totally real. Not just in my head or something. I... you... we..." She trailed off, out of adequate words.

Diana closed their eyes and heaved a heavy sigh. Their lips moved as they counted their breaths silently, regaining their composure. "I think the word you really mean is *mortal*, and the answer there would be 'Obviously not.' That's hardly relevant, though." They opened their eyes and relaxed their face. Their tone was once again light and patient. "I'm an agent of change, Emery. If change is what you want, I am happy to guide you through the ways of my kin. You found my Summoning—"

"Th-the tape?" Colleen stammered out before she could think better of interrupting. "That was—" She clamped her mouth shut when Diana raised their palms in a halting gesture.

Their eyes flashed with irritation, but their voice remained calm as they continued. "You would never have found that tape if you hadn't needed to. You took communion, and I came to see what there was to be seen. I saw that you are one of us, that you're trapped in this muted half life where no one can know you." They stepped in closer, their height suddenly matched to hers so they could stare boldly into her eyes. "You have this chance to belong, to come home and live at full volume, but only if you trust me. Unconditionally." Their mouth was a firm line, and their face completely locked down as they stepped back and waited for a response.

"I'm sorry, Diana!" Colleen frantically ran her fingers through her hair, unconsciously fluffing it as she struggled to fully display the depths of her remorse. "I don't mean to be ungrateful or disrespectful or"—she groped for the right word but gave up with a sharp shrug— "ignorant ... or whatever. Please, help me. Let me keep going. I'll do whatever it takes! Totally whatever it takes!" She implored Diana with desperate eyes, tugging on their hand with both of her own, rather than reaching out to clutch at Diana's arms like she really wanted to.

"If that's what you want," Diana replied coolly, "but we're finished for tonight."

When Colleen came to in the woods, her face was wet with tears.

he Process, as Diana had called it, continued smoothly from that point on. Colleen drank and ate whatever was offered to her without complaint and danced with joyful abandon. After a while, she noticed that her period had synched with her dreams of the clearing, and she could only wonder when exactly that had happened, just as she wondered if her dream meals had anything to do with how heavy and painful her periods had become.

Colleen groaned and hunched down in her chair, taking a moment to ride out the cramp that tore through her like an earthquake.

"My poor baby." Her mother reached over and stroked her hair tenderly. "And here I thought you might be lucky." She shook her head sadly. "Just like all the Ralston women. I'm sorry it hurts, sweetheart."

Colleen managed to throw her a grateful look even as she whimpered. "Thanks, Mom," she said weakly once the pain had passed.

Her father let his fork clatter against his plate as he glared at them and gave a disapproving *harumph*. "Save all this period talk for later. It's hardly appropriate for a nice family dinner."

Colleen mumbled a half-hearted "Sorry, Dad" while her mother rolled her eyes in an obvious, exaggerated manner before giving her husband an especially sweet smile and patting his thigh. "Excuse us, dear." She turned back to Colleen, who had gone back to her plate with relish. "I must say, sweetie, you sure have an appetite these days."

Her father laughed. "Eating us out of house and home. Do we have a daughter or a son?"

Unamused, Colleen acknowledged him with the briefest, weakest imitation of a smile. It immediately faltered back into a grimace as she barely held back from cringing at a sudden ripple of movement across her abdomen. "Ummm, excuse me, please." She eased up from the table and lurched toward the hall. She could hear her mother sadly muttering "My poor baby" as she hurried to her room. Once inside, she curled up into a ball atop her bed and buried her face into her pillow. Right on cue, she felt more movement inside herself, followed by a cramp so painful she nearly blacked out as she screamed into her pillow.

Later that night, in the clearing, she told everyone all about her dinner, but everyone seemed pleased and excited for her, rather than sympathetic. Diana clapped their hands together and nearly shouted, "Soon! It's going to happen so soon!"

"What's gonna happen?" Colleen grabbed their arm and gave their bicep a light squeeze. "What's happening to my body, Diana?"

Rather than answer, Diana took her by both arms and started them spinning. "Just dance," they said. "Let's dance together."

Soon enough, Colleen had forgotten everything. She danced, spinning in tighter and tighter circles, wearing tracks into the ground, until a cramp hit her, taking her down as if she'd been shot. She writhed on the ground, growling and whimpering in agony, forgetting everything but the persistent, throbbing tear of pain radiating up from the angry slash of her vaginal opening. Once everything had finally faded away, leaving her panting for breath, she found herself back in her own woods, dirt and twigs tangled in her hair and blood thick on her inner thighs. She carefully stood up and limped back to the house, where she sobbed silently in the shower.

The word *soon* echoed in her head, in Diana's most delighted voice, as Colleen finally reached her house. The fifteen-minute walk from school had felt more like days. The nurse had offered to call her mother at her volunteer job, but Colleen had insisted she could make it home fine. She could only laugh at herself now. She would, too, if only she weren't in such distress. She hoped that *soon* was really coming up as fast as Diana believed, because she couldn't take many more periods like this.

Holding her abdomen, Colleen lunged forward into the house. She mindlessly shoved the front door closed behind herself but didn't notice if it shut and didn't bother to check either. She was ready to drop to the floor with a loud thud, right alongside her backpack after she shrugged it off her shoulders. A new sharp shock of pain yanked a startled shout out of her, and she resisted the urge to double over. She had to get to her bedroom. She was only a few steps down the hall when she changed her mind. The thought of being inside, being confined, was too much. *This is too much pain. I need space.* She changed direction and staggered through the living room, out the glass sliding door, across the unfenced yard, past the tree line, and into the woods, where she finally allowed herself to drop in a squirming heap.

She grunted in heavy disgust when she felt an especially large, thick blood clot about to pass. Oddly, it seemed to stop halfway, as if stuck, and then there was another of the blinding, heart-stopping cramps she'd been experiencing ever since her first meal at Diana's table. Everything—the sounds of the forest around her, the grit of the dirt, rocks, and twigs under her, even the air's cheery smell—it all disappeared as the pain seized her senses. She sucked in as deep a breath as her lungs could manage and curled into herself. She tensed every muscle group to keep herself still until the torment passed. For the first time, it didn't. Instead, she could've sworn that hands slid down along her inner walls, and fingernails dug into the slick, bloody flesh before those hands began to push apart with all their might.

Even as her breath came rushing out in a tortured yelp, Colleen felt compelled to help.

She unfurled herself, wincing in agony, and pulled off her skirt and underwear. Lying on her back, oblivious to the way blood seeped down her perineum and mixed with the loose soil to form a paste that clung to her skin, she took a few long, shaky breaths to prepare. As ready as she'd ever be, she reached down, slipped four trembling fingers inside herself—two on either side—and began to pull. The whimpers and howls that erupted from her mouth as her pelvis fractured and ripped were as inhuman as the primal, animalistic growls and grunts she emitted from the effort of rending herself apart. Her own tears blinded her, and her lips were bitten and punctured, chewed completely raw, by the time she blessedly lost consciousness.

Emery emerged from the human wreckage with a determined shout, using his fingers and nails once again to grab hold, dig in, and push until he was sliding forward in a burst of blood, bile, urine, and mucus. Despite the open air and seemingly endless pines, Emery could pick out only a coppery scent so strong its warm, moist tang coated his tongue. "Ugh, it's like a full pad first thing in the morning," he muttered. He cracked his eyes open and immediately shut them again with a pained hiss. His hands were sullied with blood and dirt, so he turned back and groped about until he found his discarded skirt. He cleaned off his face and hands as well as he could and took in a deep breath of Christmas-scented air as he blinked his surroundings into slow focus. Ignoring the pile of flesh for the time being, he peered ahead, through the trees. The house was still easy to see, so he must not have made it very far before his pain overwhelmed him.

He sat and listened, appreciating the sounds of life surrounding him: birdsong, the buzz of insects flying past, the occasional twig snap or parting ferns as a small animal moved through. Eventually, he stood, and a shiver of sharp excitement traveled up his spine as the perfectly cool spring air breezed against his freshly exposed groin. Laughing, he peered down at himself and couldn't help the urge to reach down and cradle his slippery sac, recoating his hands in the waxy white secretion that covered his body. His eyes shone with tears and wonder as he tentatively tugged on his penis—giving it a couple exploratory strokes—and watched his body react. "Wow," he murmured in a delightfully deep voice. A little reluctantly, he let go of himself to run his hands up his torso, from his hips up to his clavicles, and down again. "So flat." He laughed again, feeling a little giddy when he brought his hands to rest on his pectorals. "I'm so flat."

"Happy birthday, Emery."

He turned toward the familiar voice, his lips already broadening into an ecstatic grin. "Hey, Diana!" His hands continued to travel unconsciously up and down, side to side, back and forth. He made no attempt to hide himself, or his obvious excitement, and Diana in turn made nothing of it. They merely returned his joy with a gleeful smile of their own.

"It's nice to meet you as you truly are," they offered.

The two of them stood in place, beaming at each other for a brief pause before Diana moved toward the carcass behind him, opening a burlap sack they'd been holding in one hand. "Just let me grab this," they said absently.

"You're taking it?" He watched them fit the opening of the bag over one end of his former self and begin to carefully shimmy it over the rest of the mangled remains.

Diana didn't pause as they spoke in their reassuringly authoritative tone. "You'll still need her, especially as you go through these first stages of transition." They closed the sack, heaved it up over their shoulder as if it weighed nothing, and stood. "Alright, let's go, Emery."

He looked around, not terribly keen on walking through the forest naked, and picked up his now filthy skirt. "Better than nothing," he thought aloud as he pulled it on, loving the sound of his new voice. He nodded at Diana. "I'm ready for what's next. Lead the way."

MISTER MIDNIGHT

Our house is quiet at midnight.
  My kid brother is fast asleep, tucked all snug in the quilt Mama made him, with the fluffy bear Daddy got him leaning out from inside the crook of his arm. I know because I

peek in on him every night. I just hafta know he's still here.

The floorboards would squeak, only *I* know our house too well for that. I know which spots to avoid, and anyway, I know how to be real quiet. Mama used to tell me I'm as quiet as a secret. I guess if you really tried, you might hear the funny *swiff* sound my socks make against the rug when I drag my feet.

Grammy's snores are really the only sound, and the hum of the fridge—but that you can only hear when the house is quiet like this. Grammy gets fainter as I creep down the stairs and through the first floor toward the back of the house.

I slowly slide open the glass door and step out onto the back porch before sliding the door shut again. I pull on my special going-out boots, the ones Grammy says are good for walking through the woods. I put them on and run through the yard, to the tree line Grandpa always said counts as a fence.

At midnight, the forest behind Grammy's house is quiet too.

I like it, all this quiet. Daytime is too loud. The startling, metal *clang clang clang* of Daddy's old alarm clock. The *whoosh* of the school bus door opening and closing. The bumpy rumble I feel in my feet as the bus rolls on. I always gotta pay real close attention to hear my friend Tilly over all the other kids on the bus singing, laughing, yelling, fighting. Class isn't much better. I hafta ignore all the pictures in my head and focus on the teacher, and then I always need to talk to everyone when I'd rather sit at my desk and remember what home was like, when it was the four of us.

Even at home with Grammy, where it's quieter and I feel safer. I don't mind Grammy's noise, or my kid brother's. Their noise makes me happy. But at home, my head gets to be as loud as it wants, and all the memories make me tired and they make my stomach feel like the time I ate too much cotton candy before going on the teacups ride at the state fair. In my head, there's lots of crying. Sometimes screaming. Questions I can only half remember and things I wanted to say to my brother and to Grammy but didn't know how to. Billy asking when Mama and Daddy were coming home, begging me to never leave him alone. Sometimes, it all gets so loud that my heart feels too big for my chest, my head feels like it's full of air, my skin feels like bugs are crawling all over me, and I need to crawl up into Grammy's lap and listen to her hum the same songs she used to hum to Daddy until I can breathe alright again.

That's what midnight feels like, with all its quiet. It's like making myself small in Grammy's lap, pressing my ear against her chest and hearing how calm and steady her heartbeat is, feeling her hum with my whole body and soaking up the warmth of her arms wrapping around me or her hands rubbing my back and petting my hair. This is also when I get to see my favorite friend, Mister Midnight. He's waiting for me in the woods, and he's the reason everything gets so quiet.

That night I met him, I was having trouble sleeping. My head was spinning just like the washers in the laundromat Mama used to take me to when I was real little. I felt like I was going round and round in big circles, and it made me feel hot and cranky and too awake. Then my room got cool and breezy, like I'd left my window open. The cool left as quick as it had come, but it took all the noise with it. Everything was suddenly so quiet I could hear Grammy's snores from down the hall and even the hum of the refrigerator all the way downstairs. My whole body felt lighter, and I sat up in my bed, breathing in nice and deep, like I do when I stop and smell all the wildflowers in the woods. That was when I saw him, in the corner. He's the tallest person I've ever met, even taller than Daddy was, and he's really skinny, like a twig. He dresses all in black and has hair like soot, so I probably wouldn't have noticed him, but then his skin is so pale, and his eyes glow like stars.

I know I'm supposed to be scared of strangers, and I know he shouldn't have been in my room, but I was so surprised that I forgot all that. "Did you do this?" I asked him. "Did you make it quiet?"

That made him smile, and even though his lips are thinner and paler than even Grammy's and his teeth are kinda yellow, that made me smile back.

"That's my magic," he told me. His voice is very dusty. "I can make the world quiet and calm." He moved out from the corner and stood at the foot of my bed. "You seem to need that badly." He smiled at me again, but this time I didn't smile back.

I suddenly had a great big lump of Sad in my tummy and my eyes got wet, and I had to look down at my quilt. I didn't say anything, and he stood still and silent, waiting for me.

Then I did talk. I looked back up at him and said, "Thank you for making it quiet. Will you be my friend?"

He held out his hand to me, and I took it. His skin felt like winter, but somehow it didn't make *me* cold. He helped me out of bed and let go of my hand so he could lead the way out of my room and down the stairs. We went outside, for a walk in the woods. When I asked him his name, he said, "Call me Mister Midnight, because that's when I most like to come visit."

We've gone on lots of midnight walks through the woods since then. He likes to point out how quiet the forest is and ask me if I can think of any other time when it's so silent. I never can. "It's more of my magic," he always tells me. "I make everything go still." He tells me stories as we walk, his fingers moving through the air like spiders weaving their webs. He talks a lot with his hands, just like Grandpa used to. Some of his stories are scary, some of them make me want to cry and I ask him to take me back to bed and leave me alone, but a lot of them are funny. Mister Midnight makes me laugh a lot, and I didn't know how much I missed laughing before he became my friend. I save the funniest ones to tell my brother at bedtime, and his eyes get so big, his smiles get super wide, and he laughs until he cries and tells me I'm the best sister in the whole world. Grammy laughs at them too and tells me I have such a wonderful imagination and that she's so happy to see us so cheerful. I don't tell them they're Mister Midnight's stories, because he made me promise to keep his visits a secret.

Mister Midnight is silent tonight as we walk through the woods. He's being like Tilly when she gets really upset and pretends I'm invisible. It's making me feel like caterpillars are crawling down my throat to turn into butterflies inside my tummy. All the little hairs on my arms are standing up, and my palms are sweaty. Suddenly, he stops and turns his body all the way toward me. I hafta tilt my head back to look at his face. A wide grin splits it in two, and it makes me feel so funny. It's good to see him smiling, but something about this smile makes me feel like the tummy butterflies are trying to fly up out of my mouth, past all the caterpillars crawling down. I smile back at him anyway.

"Would you like to see your parents, Sadie?"

I feel like my heart stops for a second, and then it starts to slam against my ribs. My eyes are so wide, it's like they'll fall right out of my head if I'm not careful. I'm just so excited. I'm about to jump up into Mister Midnight's arms and scream "Yes, please," but I suddenly remember Billy, sound asleep in his bed, cuddling that worn, old bear. I hold my arms stiff at my sides and curl my fingers into fists. I close my eyes and breathe slowly until my heart stops pounding. "No." I open my eyes and look up at Mister Midnight sadly. "I can't leave my baby brother. He's my favorite person in the whole world and he needs me, and I would miss him, too, if it's a long trip." I slump and take a quick look back over my shoulder, toward the house. "Would we be back by morning?"

When I look at him again, Mister Midnight's face is a little scary. He's wearing the same look Mama got that one time she caught me showing Billy how to skate across the floor on her old records and she had to turn away and count to ten before she could even talk to us. His eyes are burning like fire, and I take a few steps back. That snaps Mister Midnight out of it and he goes all nice again, but I don't trust it. I've never felt this unsure around him before, and I don't like it.

"What if I told you we could bring Billy with us?" he asks.

It's hitting me now, the same way Nancy Masters hit me that one time when she thought I'd taken her jump rope at recess. "Wait. How can you take me to see Mama and Daddy? Do you mean you'll take me to the cemetery? Grammy already does that all the time." I back up a few more steps and bump into a tree.

Mister Midnight steps toward me but doesn't get too close. He's starting to grin again. His lips are spreading slowly, wider and wider. "I'll take you to the Other Side, of course." He laughs, but it sounds mean.

I suddenly feel very cold, like being stuck outside in December wearing your summer clothes, and it gets harder to see because my eyes are too watery. I try to sound big and brave, but my voice is so small I almost can't hear myself. "You mean I have to die too?"

Mister Midnight sighs. It's the same kind of sigh I heard Mama make when she was busy and Billy wouldn't take his nap unless she kept rocking him. "I'm hungry," he says very plainly. "I've grown such an appetite, waiting for you, and I'm not going to just go away because you said no. I need to feed, one way or another." He comes another step closer, and I press my back up against the tree and whimper. "If I can't have your life and I can't eat your soul, then I suppose I can settle for your parents."

"But they're dead already," I whine.

He takes two steps back, enough for me to feel safe. "No person is fully dead as long as someone remembers them," he says in a teacher voice.

I press off the tree and step forward, scrunching my face up as I think. "You want to eat my memories?" I wipe the tears from my eyes and hug myself. I look at the ground and whisper, "I won't be able to remember Mama or Daddy ever again?"

Mister Midnight comes close and strokes my hair, the way he would have done when I still thought he was my friend. "I'll feed nice and slow; you'll hardly notice." His voice sounds nice in that same fake way all adults do when they tell you a little white lie. "Unless you think I should feed on your brother instead."

"No," I shout. I shove Mister Midnight's hand away and drop down to the ground. I curl up in a ball like a roly-poly and try so hard not to cry. I think of Mama and how she used to whisper softly into my ear when I was scared. I remember how beautiful her voice was as she sang me to sleep or whenever she was happy. I think of how Daddy always sounded a bit rough and rumbly. I told him once that his voice sounded like how his beard felt under my fingers and he laughed so hard he cried, then he kissed the top of my head and told me how much he loved me. My breaths are coming easier now, and my tears are drying up. I can even feel my mouth starting to smile.

Mister Midnight chuckles, sounding far away, and I jerk my head up to look at him. He's not there anymore. I jump up and turn in a circle, looking all around, but he's nowhere. Then I hear him again, like a rustle through the leaves of the trees. "We have a deal." With no other choice, I turn and walk back to the house.

It's getting harder and harder to hear Daddy in my head as I go up the stairs. By the time I reach my own room, I'm not sure if I can remember his voice just right and that scares me. I turn and go into Billy's room instead. I don't want to be alone.

He doesn't even wake up as I climb into his bed and give him a hug. He just tightens his hold on his teddy bear and snuggles in against me. I try not to wake him up with my crying as I try my hardest to hear Mama's voice.

The quiet isn't good anymore, but at least we're safe.

END OF THE LINE

The dream first came to her about the same time Michael fell ill. It arrived only sporadically, but never unannounced. Just as she could feel herself tilting back into the vacuum of unconsciousness, the faint yet insistent strains of piano music would worm in through her ear canals, leaving her to think *How pretty* just as she tipped all the way over into nothing.

She would wake, easing back into consciousness one observation at a time. Her ears would perk up first as they once again picked up that phantom piano. The melody would be haunting, bleak yet exquisite in its yearning melancholy. Like a soothingly hopeless nostalgia for something beyond the boundaries of human existence.

The gentle pull of fingers combing through her hair would elicit a kind of warmth that was so far removed from her usual day-to-day as to be a completely foreign sensation. Along with it came a sense of utter security and comfort. *Is this what it was like to be in the womb?* she would muse drowsily.

That was the point at which, every time, she opened her eyes and smiled up into the face of the person giving her such serenity, and that was exactly when she screamed herself fully awake.

It always took her a moment to shake off the image of the face that had greeted her adoring gaze. That grotesque display of mangled skin revealing ripped red muscle and, in some places, cracked bone. She'd force herself to forget how the thinned, stringy hair fell over the creature's shoulder, nearly touching her own sleek strands. If only that hair could've obscured the shock of that empty, endless pit of an eye socket. She'd let out a helpless whimper as she recalled how the intact eye peered down at her and how the dry, cracked lips moved in a quick, sweet smile before they moved again, exposing yellowed, brittle teeth and an obscenely parched pink tongue as they all worked together to form the sounds and words of a calming lullaby. Her skin would crawl with dread as she refused to accept how safe she had felt in those arms and how much genuine love she could read in that crystalline-blue eye.

She soon came to cringe in fear at the sound of unaccompanied piano.

In his final hour, Michael Brennan might've been alone. An only child who never did see the appeal of parenthood made widower by yet another only child, and the last one standing of his friend group. His last breath could've been unbearably lonely, indeed. But there she was.

He couldn't remember inviting her, nor could he remember hearing her come into his apartment, but she stood at his window all the same, gazing out at the gathering dusk. Her plain ivory shift dress was only a few shades off from her smooth complexion and made her charcoal hair seem all the darker as it fell down her back in slight waves. She must have sensed his wakefulness and turned away from the window to come stand at his bedside. She seemed unnaturally tall as she looked down at him, somber and attentive, but it didn't spark any fear in him.

If anything, it struck him that she felt familiar. An instinct scratching at the back of his mind told him that he knew exactly who she was and that she was no one to fear, whether he could place her or not. In any event, he was simply glad to not be alone. He forced his tired facial muscles upward into a weak smile, and with a wince of pain, unfurled the fist with which he'd been clutching the bedsheets. Body too exhausted to maneuver a whole limb, Michael only turned his hand palm up and widened his eyes pleadingly.

She perched on the edge of the bed and took his hand in hers with a heartbroken curl to her lips. She squeezed carefully and asked in a dreamlike whisper, "Does it hurt?"

"Yes," he rasped. His heart gave a feeble flutter at her glistening eyes. The gathering moisture made the icy blue of her irises appear even paler still, and never before had he seen so bereft a gaze. He understood that all that grief was solely for him, and it felt nice to be cared for again.

As if reading his mind, she pulled together the effort to offer him a full-fledged smile. It lasted only a moment before she asked, keeping her tone soft and compassionate, "Are you afraid, Michael?"

He watched her curiously, vaguely noting how much he was starting to relax and how even his pain was slowly receding. He blinked, somewhat startled to find his eyes watery, and cleared his throat. "Not with you here." His dry voice creaked like settling floorboards. Growing weary, he closed his eyes. A flush of memories suddenly overwhelmed him: the sweet love and comfort of his mother's lullabies, the glorious sound of his husband's absent-minded humming as he cooked. *Exactly what I need*, he thought. He didn't bother opening his eyes to look at his visitor as he made his request. "Sing me to sleep?"

She blinked away the tears that had welled up in the inner corners of her eyes and took in a deep breath. She released it slowly and squared her shoulders against the sorrow that wanted to drop down and crush her into the floor. She gave his hand one last gentle squeeze and moved to stroke what snowy hair was left atop his head. She gathered up all her sadness with one more deep breath and channeled it into her song.

Somehow, she failed to note the familiarity of the tune.

She returned to her own lodgings, after bearing witness to Michael's transition to the world beyond life, and startled with a harsh gasp upon reaching her bedroom door. She instinctively gripped her throat, as if that could keep her panic at bay. A monstrous figure sat daintily on the edge of her bed, watching her expectantly. They had folded back her quilt and fluffed her pillow, and now they merely sat up tall and straight, smiling patiently.

She swallowed down her unease and took a few tentative steps forward, taking in the same exact face she had been seeing in her dreams and moving her gaze down to catalog the black satin tunic that blessedly covered up most of what she could tell was a mutilated frame of bone, muscles, and skin that somehow held itself together.

She cleared her throat and stammered, uncertain, "D-Death? Is it you?"

Death chuckled warmly. "Who else could I be, dear child?"

She came to sit beside them finally, no longer feeling afraid. "I've been dreaming of you lately," she whispered, suddenly shy. "Why are you here?"

They placed a hand on her cheek, as if giving her a motherly kiss. The skin was leathery, and the bone chilled her skin where it touched. Death grinned, the gruesome sight somehow giving off an aura of great affection. "At the end of the line, even the banshee earns her rest." Death pulled their hand away and patted the bed before standing up to give her a chance to get comfortable.

Feeling an inexplicable sense of relief and reward, she got under the covers. She turned her face into the pillow as Death tucked her in. Her nostrils flared to take in the calming scent of vanilla and fresh-churned butter—olfactory remnants of a bustling kitchen from a life as long ago and forgotten as the banshee's original name. It coaxed her lips into a tender smile as she glanced back to meet Death's serene gaze for just a moment.

They merely hummed awhile as they stroked the banshee's hair, strands sometimes catching on chipped bone. By the time they began to sing their ethereal lullaby, her face had already relaxed into stillness and her chest just barely moved with the lessening effort of ever-weakening breaths.

Having foretold, witnessed, and mourned generations upon generations of death, the Brennan Banshee met her own end with a comfortable warmth that eased through her like a slow, smooth sleep.

ESTRANGED

I don't grieve my parents. There was a time when I certainly would've. At one point, I loved them and felt loved in return. All I feel now, as I look through the family photo albums—some of the very few things I bothered to take from their house before I hired all manner of people to deal with the responsibilities I don't care for—is a nagging sense of obligation that somehow didn't die along with them, an ever-present undercurrent of resentment, and a growing bewilderment.

Looking at all the photos Mom so lovingly pasted onto the pages of her "retro chic" leather-bound albums makes me realize, again, just how strange my memory is. Or maybe it's no stranger than anyone else's. I don't really know. Things like childhood memories would be a bit faded, wouldn't they? Mine seem worse than that, though. Crude pencil drawings with colors so muted they may as well be grayscale. They never change either. Isn't that a thing? Don't people naturally change up their stories? A forgotten detail might resurface or one might get lost, how the memory's shared might change based on how you feel in the moment— all those tiny, unconscious tweaks. The cave wall etchings in my mind never shift, never develop any kind of nuance.

Even my teenage years have that suspicious flatness to them. You'd think, if nothing else, at least puberty would be a jumble of bold, Technicolor scenes that play over and over. Not for me. My memory doesn't become vivid until I was seventeen, and the difference would steal your breath. It jolts from that washed-out chicken-scratch art to color and detail worthy of the Sistine Chapel. It's even a bit of a joke between me and the rest of the English Department how my memory is eerily photographic.

This picture here. My brother curled into my side as I read him a story. I can recall it well enough to tell you about it. I was twelve, so he must've been seven. We were both sick with some kind of bug. I was already on the mend, and he'd just caught it. I read to him every night until he got better. I can't *feel* this memory, though. I can't tell you if I felt guilty about getting him sick or if I just enjoyed mothering him. I can't tell you if his skin was warm or clammy, if the blanket pulled up over him felt itchy or soft against my bare shins. I can only guess based on what I see here, and if you ask me, the photograph is lying. Sean looks too happy. He's cuddled up to me too tightly, his body language is too relaxed, and he's looking at me with too much love and admiration. Maybe when we were twelve and seven, it was different; but I can tell you with absolute certainty that the Sean I remember well has always hated everything about me. Every picture in these earlier albums tells the same lie: a proud, affectionate sister and the little brother that thinks she hung the moon. Memory after memory that I can pull out of my personal data bank but can't—not for the life of me—attach to any particular sense or emotion.

The tawny album makes a satisfying, soft little *thump* as I close it. I push it off my lap and reach for the cherry red one next. If I recall correctly, this one houses a lot of my teenage years. Flipping through the first few pages, it's odd that there aren't any pictures of me from ages fourteen through sixteen. I'm hard pressed to remember anything from then too. I've had friends, lovers, and therapists alike suggest to me that my brain is possibly blacking out some kind of trauma. I'm not saying that I disagree, but I can't seem to access that hypothetical trauma or any shoddy, partially formed memories. Three years just seemingly gone forever. If I were desperate to solve the mystery, I could always book a weekend at one of those Neuro Spas and get a HippoLift. I'm not though, or to be perfectly honest, I can't afford to be. So, the only people who have any idea about those lost years are either recently deceased or haven't talked to me since they left home to work with our uncle.

When I think of my family, I always feel like I've got things backward. There's no instinct in me to mourn the literal dead, but the loss I feel when I think of Sean living a whole entire life that I'm not privy to permeates every part of my own. I'm tempted to open the tawny album again and do a side-by-side comparison of the memories I know as if by rote and the ones I can feel deep in my gut. I don't know if I really have the strength for that, though, seeing an adorably happy, loving little brother up against the angry, defiant, spiteful one.

More than anything in this world, I wish I understood what happened. I wish I knew how and when everything went wrong. Each one of those pictures—where the two of us are laughing together or grinning ear to ear, arms around each other as we look to the camera, each candid shot where Sean is looking at me like I could do no wrong or I'm looking at him like he's the best gift my parents ever gave me— is a dull, rusty knife twisting in my heart.

They remind me how the entire English Department knows not to mention my family, ever. Even our department chair, who has a notoriously rocky relationship with her sister, stopped trying to commiserate with me once she realized how jealous I was of their problems. The scant friends I have, they've learned to treat their own siblings like their dirtiest secret. If I'm honest, that's probably the main reason I find friendships so fleeting, on the odd occasion I manage to properly forge them. Who wants to constantly hide their loved ones from someone meant to be counted among them?

I've tried reaching out to Sean over the years, of course, through our uncle. I wouldn't say I have a relationship with Uncle Jerry, only that he takes my phone calls even when it's not his birthday or a major holiday, and I'm grateful. He never has anything new to tell me about Sean, though, and never fails to advise me to stop asking because, as he always puts it, "Sean ain't interested, and it ain't my place to give out his anything." My last phone call was the only exception he ever made, and it still didn't garner me any information. He only promised to make sure Sean knew about the funeral.

"Can't imagine he'll care a whit," he mused, "but I suppose it's only right to tell 'im. Just don't get your hopes up thinking he'll come, and don't expect me there neither." There'd been an awkward pause, and then he offered me one last thing before he hung up, all his usual gruffness completely gone. "Sorry for your loss, Emily."

It was such a strange experience, attending that funeral. I'm surprised I even went, but in the end, I couldn't shake off that sense of duty to be a good daughter. The church was a room of strangers: friends and acquaintances of my parents' that I knew by name, and only vaguely, because they'd come into Mom and Dad's life after I'd left home. None of the cousins, who I had lost touch with anyway. Not any of Dad's sisters, and of course, no Uncle Jerry. No family friends I remember from childhood. My parents did have a knack for alienating people. The people that were in attendance were not especially kind either. There was lots of tongue clucking and hissed whispers behind hands, lots of long looks boring into me when my back was turned. Especially in the past few years, my parents had a certain zeal in telling everyone all about their miserable, ungrateful children. The son that had left without so much as a "thanks for nothing" as soon as he graduated from high school, and the daughter that held them at a very icy arm's-length but was all too happy to accept help when she needed it. They made sure to omit the fact that I'd not asked them for help of any kind since my early twenties.

It was just as I had finally given up and slipped out the front doors, to leave them all to their gossip, that I saw him. Sean was leaning against a tree out in the courtyard, hands shoved in his pockets, shoulders slumped, and face as surly as ever. The sheer shock of knowing he'd come felt like a momentary shutdown, and I stood frozen in place until our eyes met and he blanched as if he'd seen a ghost.

"I've been meaning to find you," he said when we met each other halfway, "but I kept changing my mind at the last minute." He shrugged, glancing down at the ground briefly. "You see, there's someone I want you to meet." Nerves exploded all over his face as he said that. His shoulders hunched forward, and he broke eye contact again. A blush briefly bloomed across his cheeks, immediately piquing my interest. "Someone important to me," he said as he scuffed his shoe against the grass. "Eli. He really wants to meet you."

I didn't bother questioning the why, or the timing, or anything, really. Truthfully, I didn't care. All that mattered at that moment was the fact I was finally getting the second chance I've always wanted. So, Sean and I exchanged ChitChapp IDs and parted ways for the time being with no small amount of awkwardness. I'm not sure how Sean felt walking away from that interaction, but I left that day with an excited little flutter of hope.

And now it's time to head out to the café and see if that bit of hope making my palms sweaty is foolish or not.

A refreshing breeze cools my face as I trace the trail left by a drop of condensation on the side of my glass. I'm glad I sat outside. The last thing I need when I'm already feeling this anxious is to feel closed in on all sides by a crowd. "That really wasn't the best idea," I mumble down at the half-eaten croissant in front of me. I thought, when I got here half an hour sooner than necessary, that some food might settle me. Instead, it's sitting heavy in my stomach as I wait for Sean to come back out with his drinks. Eli came separately, and he has yet to arrive. An urge to dash to the bathroom and check my face for the zillionth time is rising up from my gut. It feels annoyingly like the need to pee, but I'm not being fooled again. "You'll be okay. Everything's fine." Before I have a chance to either breathe my way through the nerves or start spiraling, Sean appears and sits across from me, putting down two large to-go cups. So, then, he's not expecting to stay long either. That's somehow comforting. Eyeing that second cup, I wonder if Eli just happened to ask Sean to order for him or if Sean has a reason to know this mystery man's go-to drink order.

"So, who is Eli?" I can't help but perk up as I meet my brother's gaze. "A boyfriend?" The prospect makes me smile despite our estrangement, but then a new thought jumps out, and I start to feel bad as I piece it together. "Is that why you left home as soon as you could? Because Mom and Dad wouldn't accept that you're gay?"

Sean tenses up, his mouth making the same tight, downward curve I can feel forming across my own face.

"That doesn't seem right, since they got so obsessive over—"

"No, Emily. Just stop." He straightens up aggressively, nearly standing up out of his chair, and flattens his palms against the tabletop, splaying his fingers out wide. A passerby pauses and shoots us a concerned look before deciding they don't want to be involved and walking on.

Startled, I snap my mouth shut and blink at him.

He takes a deep breath and forces himself to drop the hostile body language. He speaks carefully, like he's reciting a prepared statement. "I left because I hated them, full stop. Uncle Jerry offered me a real home with real family and a real future."

I quickly swallow down the urge to insist *we* were a real family and drop my gaze down to the table. "I'm sorry, Sean. I didn't mean to upset you." I look back up at him meekly.

His shoulders drop a little, and his mouth loses some of its tightness.

"I'm just nervous and I was a bit excited, I guess." A sigh escapes and I shrug helplessly, reaching out to trail my fingertip along my glass again. I make sure I'm looking him straight in the eye, so he can see the earnestness in mine. "I would've felt honored to be introduced to someone as important as a partner."

His entire body deflates as he lets out his own sigh. He looks down and stares at the cup in front of him. He grabs it and takes a drink. I'm surprised to recognize it as one of his old stall tactics from when we were younger. I guess you just don't forget things like that, regardless of how close you are to someone. "I'm sorry, okay." He puts his drink down and looks back at me. "He's told me himself I need to be kinder to you. I apologize for jumping down your throat." He gives a lazy, half shrug and sits back in his chair. "If you really must know, I'm never going to be introducing you to any kind of partner. I'm not interested."

Grateful for the crumb, I smile at him and lean slightly forward. "Oh, so you're asexual?"

He rolls his eyes and scoffs, making me cringe because I'm already so sick of putting my foot wrong with him. "I'll tell you one thing you've got in common with Russ and Leah." I wince at hearing their actual names instead of *Dad* and *Mom*, but Sean doesn't notice. "You sure seem obsessed with sex and gender."

A flare of irritation shoots up my spine, and I can't stop myself from glaring at him, which elicits a fleeting look of surprise. "Now, wait a minute," I demand. "That's not really fair." I cross my arms over the table, clutching at my own elbows, and lean in toward him. "Look, Sean. I know you don't like me." I abruptly rein myself in, just enough to keep my temper. My voice softens a little as I continue. "I don't understand why, and I'm not here to find out either. I just want to— I'm trying to—" I need to pause and collect my thoughts. I loosen my grip on my arms and fix him with a pleading look that seems to ease some of the harshness in his face. "I figured that since you invited me here, you might want to have a relationship with me. I'd like that. I'm just trying to be your sister, and it feels like a safe assumption to make, that you're introducing me to your partner given the suddenness of it all." I sit back, tossing my hands up in the air briefly. "And okay, it probably really isn't any of my business, your sexuality, but it seemed a natural continuation to the conversation. I'm sorry, okay? I'm sorry. I just want to chat with you like a normal person."

He looks laughably guilty, but only for a moment before he steels himself and offers a placating smile. "Okay, okay." He holds up his hands, palms out in a surrendering gesture. "I'm sorry too. I don't need to be so snippy; I get it." He nods, as if trying to reinforce the message for himself. "No, it's not that big a deal to me for people to know, so I didn't need to jump down your throat. Yeah. I'm aroace." He leans back again, crossing his arms over his chest and eyeing me with a raised brow. "What about you?"

"I—" Instantaneously, I realize that what I was about to say isn't exactly true. "You know. I'm not too sure I know." I can feel the confusion stealing across my face as I puzzle it out aloud for the first time. "I mean, I know I'm not asexual . . . I don't think." Genuine interest sparks in Sean's eyes as he shifts closer. "It's been a while since I've been with someone because . . ." I need another pause to think of what I mean, to flip back through my catalog of past relationships. I take a sip of water as he takes a sip of whatever he ordered. We set our drinks down at the same time. "It all started feeling too much like I was just trying to meet expectations."

Empathy darkens the amber of his eyes, taking me aback because it's not something I've ever seen him exhibit—not for me. "Whose expectations?" he asks in an uncharacteristically soft tone.

"Mom and Dad. After a while, it felt like it didn't matter what I felt or who I was, or what made me happy, or anything like that. The only thing that mattered was whether I was the child they wanted, and those parameters seemed to shift constantly."

Sean's face has gone moody again, but I get the feeling he's thinking, really taking my words into consideration, and trying to formulate a response. Before he can figure it out, his body language shifts again, becoming soft and loose. He perks up in his chair, and his eyes light up as he raises a hand. "Over here."

I turn around, and my body acts of its own accord, springing up out of my chair and taking small steps forward. I swear, my heart has stopped. I've forgotten how to breathe. I can only stare with big, dumbstruck eyes and a gaping mouth. I'm looking at fair skin that favors our mother. I'm looking at a prominent beauty mark in the exact same spot as the one I have just below my right eye. There's a scar going through the left eyebrow, if I were to guess—and I'm infinitely confident doing so—it's from falling off the couch at age five and splitting his forehead open. I'm looking at brown hair so light that, depending on the lighting, it could trick you into thinking it's strawberry blond. Unsurprisingly, I'm the exact same height as this man, or I would be if I had worn my flats. He's broader than me, with a thicker neck and a more chiseled jawline. I don't realize I've started moving back again until I bump into my chair and practically collapse into it. I'm still focused on his face, my head tilted back so I can keep looking into his eyes. Eyes that can seem more brown or more green, depending on his mood. As I watch them turn muddy, I know for a fact my own eyes are doing the same.

"Wow, it's uncanny," he says in a deeper version of my voice, with the exact same inflection I would've used. "I guess you're my sister?" He lets out a rumbly version of my nervous laugh. "It feels too weird to say that you're me."

"H-How? How could I be you?" I finally jerk my gaze away, refusing to look as I sense him move closer and take a seat between me and Sean. "Why wouldn't it be the other way around?" I'm feeling lightheaded now, dizzy with confusion, and the pounding of my heart is too loud and so distracting. I turn back and frown at him, hyperaware of how my lips are moving to form my expression. "Maybe you're me!" I hear a hint of impending hysteria in my voice. I wonder if they notice it too.

"Don't you get it?" Sean interjects, irritated with me again. I whip my head around to face him, beginning to feel like a cornered animal. Sitting outside didn't help as much as I thought it would. "You're not real, Emily," he practically shouts.

"Wh-what does that even mean?" I finally blink. I blink several times and grab my water. It feels so strange, pouring down my throat as I chug. It's not helping me calm down, that's for sure. Feeling uncoordinated, I accidentally slam the glass down, making what's left near the bottom wobble angrily. I'm surprised I didn't shatter the glass. I stare dumbly at my hand, still curled around it, and speak slowly. "How could I not be real?"

Sean drags his fingers through his hair roughly, frustrated. "I just mean—"

Eli stills him with a gentle pat on the shoulder and looks at me, waiting for me to focus as best I can on his eerie face. "You weren't born, Emily." He's speaking in my signature soft tone, the one I use to sound sympathetic and big-hearted when I have to relay bad news. "Our mother never carried you. You were manufactured."

"When Eli ran away from home, our shit-tastic parents tried to just replace him." Sean forces his way back into the conversation, making me jump. Eli frowns sympathetically, even looks like he wants to reach out and take my hand, but Sean doesn't notice and barrels on. "You're a fucking clone, Emily!"

My vision implodes, narrowing down to a tiny pinprick of light before it all goes black, and I'm left in this eye-aching darkness with my heavy heartbeat jackhammering into my eardrums. I think death may be better than this.

A splash of cold brings the world back into view and I gasp wildly. Slowly, I realize Eli is holding my hand and talking to me. He's directing me to breathe. I follow his directions as he tells me, "Breathe in. Hold for one, two, three, four. Breathe out." My pulse eventually settles, and I regain my awareness little by little. It looks like Sean splashed the last of my water in my face, to get me out of whatever space I was in. He's flushed, holding my glass, and wearing the guiltiest expression I've ever seen on anyone. The other outside tables have crowded around. I scan the strange faces, not really making eye contact with anyone, and offer the most convincing smile I can manage.

Sean clears his throat. "Okay, people. She's alright. Move on, already." Grudgingly, the small crowd disperses, and Sean takes his seat again, putting my glass down on the table. I wiggle my fingers and Eli takes the hint, letting go of me so that I can wipe the moisture away from my eyes and grab a tissue from my purse to dab at my face.

"So." I look from Eli to Sean, silently asking for an explanation. "I'm a..." I can't finish this sentence. It's too bizarre.

Sean sighs. "Eli ran away when I was nine." He blinks rapidly, and I realize he's trying not to tear up.

Eli reaches over and rubs his shoulder soothingly, almost like he's offering an apology Sean's heard and accepted countless times already.

Sean nods and sucks in his lower lip, chewing on it for a moment before he continues. "When that happened—" He takes a deep breath and holds it for a moment. His body is tensing up again. "Those sick bastards didn't even look for him." He shakes his head in disgust.

I can feel that same disgust brewing in the pit of my stomach. How could they not even care that their child had run away? I glance at Eli. He's staring down at his hands, folded together on the tabletop. I can read the deep-seated pain in the sag of his shoulders and neck so easily because it's my very own body language I'm looking at right now. Disturbed, I look back to Sean instead. "They took out loans, drained their savings, stole our college funds." His eyes ignite with anger. "They did what they felt they had to do to get the money together, and then they went to that place." His nostrils flare, and he spits out his next words. "Facsimile Limited."

"They didn't love me." Eli sighs. He slowly raises his head and meets my gaze.

I'm almost numb with shock and simply listen.

"They couldn't accept the fact that I was their son. They tried to force me to be the daughter they expected, that they insisted I really was." One of my own morbid smirks flashes across his face.

"So, they thought they'd just try again, then?" I barely recognize my voice as I share that thought aloud. It sounds somehow both fragile and robotic.

"Yeah," Sean snorts. "They figured no better way to get a daughter that would meet their expectations."

"But." I blink, stare down at my own hands as I open and close my fists. My own skin feels so strange. "But they—" I look up and catch Eli's eyes. Looking into them, I know exactly how pained and dark my own are right now. "In the end, they just tried to turn me into the son that had run away instead of the daughter they thought they wanted."

Sean's eyes darken with disgust and that old, familiar disdain I grew up with. It's just more strangeness, to see it there and know that it's not meant for me.

I switch my gaze over to Eli. His thick, ashy brows slant down, and his eyes well with empathy. The kind of piteous understanding that can only come from someone who was raised by the same parents as you. "I know, Emily, I know. They didn't love me first." He huffs out a frustrated breath and shakes his head in what I can instinctively tell he would like to be disbelief instead of resignation. "So, it took them ruining a whole other child to figure out I deserved to be loved for me."

Sean grunts. "Sounds exactly like them."

"Emily." Eli straightens up, gives the same nearly imperceptible little shake I do when I'm trying to get my bearings and shift focus. He smiles encouragingly at me. "The reason I wanted to meet you is, well . . ." He glances over at Sean and Sean gives a slight nod. "I'd really like for us to have a relationship. I mean, for all intents and purposes, you *are* my twin sister."

An odd, gasping laugh of shock and excitement bursts past my lips, and I blurt out, "Really? Siblings? Like, proper siblings that like each other and keep up with one another?" I slap my cheeks, rubbing the sting into them as I turn my wide eyes on Sean. "Even you? You really want this?"

He blushes, looking disarmingly sheepish. "Yeah, well, I guess it would be nice." He grabs his cup and takes a long sip. He has a difficult time meeting my gaze as he sets it down and finishes his thought. "I guess it's not like, your fault or anything. You didn't take my brother away from me."

"Of course it's not her fault." Eli grins at him and ruffles his hair. A sudden jealousy and longing prick my heart as I read all the love in the interaction. "Emily asked to be made just as much as either of us asked to be born. It's all on Mother and Father."

"Right, right. I know." Sean offers me a timid smile. "I'd like to try. I promise to do my best."

I think back to all those pictures that I now know to be of Eli and Sean. The warm, easy affection that shines beyond the frame. I'd like that. I really would. I'm just now realizing exactly how lonely I've felt all my life, how desperately I've clung to labels like *girlfriend* and *daughter* and *professor*, just to keep myself oblivious to that feeling of being completely adrift in the universe, and it's crushing.

But how could I?

I notice that my mouth is hanging open and snap it shut. A high-pitched ringing assaults my eardrums and I squeeze my eyes closed. There's a warm, tentative touch on my shoulder. It must be Eli. I assume he's saying something to me, but it's like he's not really here. We're not on the same plane as I reach up and press my fingers against my temples, uselessly massaging them while the doubts gain real traction in my head and my pulse speeds up to match that nauseating tone in my ears.

How could I be around Eli? I'd always be analyzing how we're the same, how we're maybe different. Only, I'd never truly be able to know *if* we're any different, would I? Is it *really* possible for a clone to deviate from the source material? How could I have Eli in my life and still maintain a sense of my own validity?

My mind is flooding with those pictures again. All those lies. Because I was right, after all. They are lies, every last one. They aren't telling me the story of my beautiful sibling relationship that somehow went sour. All this time, they've been mocking me with the beautiful relationship that Eli had with his brother, the one I never had, and all things considered, never will have. To Sean—even if we find our footing somehow, even if he's just said he understands I'm not at fault, I'm always going to be the abomination that tried to take his brother's place. In the depths of his heart, I'm always going to be a poorly made copy. How could Eli really want this? If the roles were reversed, I'm not too sure I would ever get used to treating my clone like a brother. I'm not sure I'd ever feel at ease. How? How could Mom and Dad have done this to us?

The scream of pressure that was building up in my head dramatically releases when the shrill ringing abruptly stops and the ambient sounds of my surroundings filter back in. I blink my eyes open to discover my face is wet with tears, and I'm panting from the effort of forcing my breaths to keep coming. Finally registering the muscle tension of my hunched form, I force myself to relax and sit up straight in my chair. Eli is watching me with compassionate worry, and even Sean looks genuinely concerned. He shifts in his chair, pulls at the collar of his shirt as if he's trying to breathe easier, and clears his throat. "Uh, Emily? Are you okay?"

Still feeling dazed, I shake my head slowly and work on taking deep, centering breaths. I'm trying to dislodge this growing sense of detachment, but it's not working. I scan the sidewalk, take note of the people passing by, watch traffic crawl past on the road as it comes to a stop at the traffic light. I hear a sudden laugh from the table to our left, and I can't help but notice how canned it sounds. Like a laugh track on an old sitcom.

"Yeah," I finally say slowly. I lock gazes with Sean across the table, but he seems exaggerated somehow. Like an actor playing Sean. "Yeah, I'm—I'm okay." I turn to my left and try to smile at Eli. The way the fine lines in his face deepen tells me I'm not convincing anyone. "Look, guys." I force out a laugh. "I really appreciate this little coffee date." I glance over at Sean and try another smile before looking back to Eli. "And I appreciate what you're offering so much." I reach out to grab a hand from both of them and offer a quick squeeze, the movement feeling oddly mechanical. "I need some time to think, though. Can I get back to you?" I look across the table. "Sean?"

Eli answers for them in our softest, most encouraging tone. "Of course, Emily. You take all the time you need; we can wait for you."

I get up awkwardly. Probably, they were about to leave, and maybe I should've let them be the ones to go, but I need to do something, need to have some sense of control. My body easily goes through the motions of a polite goodbye—facial muscles pulling my lips up at the corners and making soft creases at the corners of my eyes. My vocal cords vibrate and work with my lips, teeth, and tongue to form words my brain isn't really registering. Instead, my head is all static as I walk away, ballooning up with pressure until I don't trust anything: the impact as my heels click against the sidewalk, the pull of fabric against my thighs as I walk, the brush of my purse against my side, the various smells that waft past my nose as I pass different stores and narrowly avoid bumping into people. The city noise surrounding me is drowned out by that fuzzy buzz in my head. I just don't know about anything anymore, so I keep walking. Maybe, if I walk for long enough, I'll start to feel real again. Real enough to make myself a life that's all mine, even if I end up living it all on my own.

KIDS SAY THE DARNDEST THINGS

It had been blessedly easy to move Lucy into her own room. She loved her princess bed, the lavender polka-dot curtains she picked out all by herself, her cheery Hello Kitty nightlight. All in all, the rambunctious toddler seemed anxious to reach Big-Girl status. Only every so often did Lucy need an extra hug, a glass of water, or an urgent safety check under the bed and in the closet.

But that easy transition, it seemed, reached an end three days ago. It was only Wednesday now, and Joyce and Nate felt they'd had enough bedtime tantrums, nightmare freak-outs, and bed invasions to last them well beyond the end of the week.

"What do you think is wrong? What on earth happened?" Joyce put her book down on her bedside table and watched her husband climb into bed.

Nate clicked off the lamp on his own bedside table and scooted closer to her. "I dunno, babe." He linked his fingers through hers with one hand and scratched down her back with the other. He smiled to himself as he felt Joyce relax into his touch and continued in a low, soothing tone. "She's only two. It's probably just a phase. Maybe being all by herself in her big-girl room is catching up to her."

"Hmmm . . ." Joyce nuzzled against him for a moment before reaching over to turn off her lamp. "I hope so." She pulled him down so they could nestle into each other's warmth. "Let's hope we can actually sleep tonight."

The first wake-up came just after midnight. The abrupt whimper and ragged breathing over the baby monitor woke Joyce. Luckily, a quick snuggle and a short lullaby was all Lucy needed to get back to sleep.

Nate was the next to go in a couple hours later. He was able to soothe their daughter with nothing more than a reassuring back rub and a kiss on the forehead.

When Lucy woke up sobbing sometime after three, Joyce and Nate agreed there was nothing to do but bring her back into their bed.

Joyce couldn't help but shiver and hug herself tightly as she stepped into Lucy's room. "Poor baby," she cooed as she bent down and lifted a watery-eyed, sniveling Lucy out of her bed. "It's freezing in here." Oblivious to the snotty wetness as Lucy buried her face in her neck, Joyce crossed over to the window to confirm it was properly shut and latched. Her body stiffened with unease when she saw that it was, and that hot air was indeed coming in through the heater vent. The realization taunted her mind, convincing her something was breathing down her neck as she hustled out of the room.

She carried Lucy into the kitchen where she hummed and swayed until her little girl finally relaxed in her arms. After quick sip of water and a chance to use the bathroom, mother and daughter settled into bed rather easily. Nate, as expected, was already sound asleep and snoring.

Joyce wasn't sure when or why she woke up. She hadn't even been aware of any shift in states of consciousness. She was simply awake. Her eyes tried to adjust to the darkness, but ultimately failed. In the dead of the night, in the middle of winter, the primary bedroom became like a cavern, an infinite darkness that seemed to swallow her up. She cowered despite herself, the same way she used to when she was a child and still afraid of the dark.

In the middle of that blackness, right at her side, Lucy's whispering voice suddenly broke the eerie silence. Joyce couldn't make out a single syllable. All she could tell was that Lucy was turned away from her, and whatever was happening, the little girl was clearly amused. Giddy giggles interrupted the hushed words. At first, Joyce assumed that her daughter was talking in her sleep. Nate had the habit. He often said the most ludicrous, entertaining things while dreaming. The thought did nothing to console her, however. The inexplicable fear in her gut continued to crawl up through her body, suggesting that this was entirely different.

What is she dreaming of? What is she talking about?

Joyce rolled fully onto her side and went to wrap her hand around Lucy's arm to give it a careful shake and ask who she was talking to. She snatched her hand back with a sharp gasp, shocked at the iciness of her daughter's skin.

The silence was immediate and alarmingly absolute. Though it was only a moment, it felt like eons crawled past before Joyce felt her little girl's body shifting and then felt her breath puff out against her. It was just as chilled as Lucy's skin, making Joyce shiver. Then, Lucy reached up and stroked her cheek, her coldness making Joyce's teeth chatter.

Finally, Lucy said in her sweetest, most delighted voice, "Yay. Yay. Yay. You're gonna die."

Hearing such sophisticated language roll so smoothly out of her two-year-old's mouth set off the final alarm bells in Joyce's mind, and she choked on air. Forcing herself to speak through the panic that had her throat constricting and her heart slamming against her ribcage, Joyce hissed, "What have you done with my daughter?"

Lucy shifted again, pushing Joyce onto her back with alarming strength and then sitting cross-legged on her chest. Her small, two-year-old body somehow put enough pressure on Joyce's chest that all the air whooshed out of her lungs, and her vision faded and grew fuzzy around the edges as the chill emanating from Lucy shocked her body into stillness.

"Shhh." Lucy leaned forward, covering her mother's mouth and clamping her nose with that impossible strength. "Time to be quiet, Mommy."

I'LL NEVER LEAVE YOU

With its crisp robin's-egg blue siding, clean white trim, and violet front door, the house had practically jumped out from the online listing, and Marisol had needed to see it in person as soon as possible.

The simply upholstered porch swing seemed to invite Marisol straight up from the street to relax in the shade of the overhang as she sipped from a steaming mug of perfectly blended coffee. She knew her son would be delighted in the alternating snapdragons and lady's slippers that flanked the stonework path to the front porch, and James was already making plans for a little herb garden by the time they saw the backyard. Marisol loved everything about the house, from its real hardwood floors and newly carpeted bedrooms to its renovated kitchen and surprisingly high ceilings. It was that bold, beautiful door, however, she kept coming back to.

"Purple doors are supposed to invite opportunities," she mused as they all followed the Realtor over the threshold and back out into the front yard.

The Realtor laughed good-naturedly and added, "Purple's also been considered the color of royalty for, gosh, since forever. Right?" She turned then and winked at her clients, practically sealing the deal. Marisol knew right then exactly what 117 Vine Street was meant to be: her new beginning.

Slowly but surely, in the first months of life behind that purple door, Marisol began collecting up the bits and pieces of herself that had been chipped away over the past three years. With every morning that she managed to greet the day without a sinking feeling deep in her gut, and every mundane task she found herself completing with more and more frequency, Marisol had felt her soul mending itself and her mind strengthening.

It was when she had finally begun to embrace her life again that evil found her.

Marisol knelt comfortably in the gentle spring sun, tucking the last of her gladiolus corms into the soil and thus finishing off the bordering trim of plant life she'd planned for the front of the house. She couldn't wait for summer to arrive so she could witness the staggered reveal of white, pink, burgundy, and pale green. As she tamped down the soil and set her trowel aside, she thought she heard a sibilant whisper of "Pssst, pssst" in the exact intonation her mother had always used to get her attention, and which she now used as a mother herself.

Dazed curiosity washed over her as she glanced over her shoulder. Her eyes caught on a petite woman with the same warm, moreno skin as her mother as they made their way down the street. Their hair seemed to steal all the sunlight for itself, to better bring out its soft, caramel highlights. There was something slow and methodical about the way they moved. Marisol couldn't shake the feeling that they were making sure she noticed them, and now that they had her full attention, they stopped. In the blink of an eye, they seemed to travel the remaining distance to stand just feet away from Marisol on her stone pathway. They stood regally with their head held high and their hands gently clasped in front of them as they waited. Waited for what, Marisol was unsure.

Too anxious to get up, Marisol merely straightened her back and tilted her head toward them. She tried not to let her voice waver as she asked, "Can I help you?"

A loose-lipped, sharp-edged smirk slipped across their face while their eyes narrowed and seemed to flash. Marisol's pulse pounded in her ears as her fretful gaze locked with their expectant glare. A painful spark zipped through her brain, and her mouth fell open with a silent gasp as she remembered.

The details were incomplete in the way remembered nightmares often were, but all the same, they stuck into her like jagged shards of glass. A dinner party at her mother's house, every person she'd ever known, dazzling lights, disorienting conversation, then a deep darkness, only Marisol and the one single stranger in attendance, a bone-crushing grip on Marisol's wrist and a dark promise hissed into her ear. "I'll see to it your baby is never born."

The air rushed out of Marisol's lungs in the form of a startled cry as the mysterious woman seemed to vanish completely. Her lower abdomen clenched in phantom pain, stealing her breath yet again, and Marisol folded into herself. Moist soil transferred from her gardening gloves to her blouse when she gripped her stomach. She tucked her head in and squeezed her eyes shut against the tears that wanted to form. Screams bubbled and boiled in her diaphragm but died before she could expel them. She lost the battle against her own misery and let the sobs come instead. Her tears streaked her cheeks and mingled with the dirt, sullying her face.

Whoever or whatever that woman had been, they'd dredged up the worst dream Marisol had ever had in her life: The one she'd had only a matter of days before she'd miscarried at twelve weeks. The cold, clinical confirmation of the ultrasound technician at the emergency room had been devastating, and the pain that followed, agony of so many varieties, unbearable. Her reliably superstitious mother had only made matters worse by, as an attempt at comfort, insisting that Marisol had fallen prey to a manananggal. It had felt disgustingly offensive to take her suffering and try to explain it away with some grisly tale of a vampiric monster slurping up her baby straight from the womb.

Warm, gentle hands cupping her face and tender lips pressing against her forehead brought Marisol back to herself, and she slowly blinked her husband into focus. His eyes narrowed in scrutiny, but his pupils expanded to take in more of her as he carefully searched her face with a disquieted expression clearly etched into his own. "What's the matter?" The pads of his thumbs stroked across her skin as he lovingly wiped away the dirt and tears.

She sniffled and offered him a weak smile. "I . . . uh"—her lips tightened and her gaze faltered for a moment—"remembered something sad." She gave herself away with an unconscious rub of her belly, and his gaze dropped to track the movement. The usually bright, clear amber of his eyes seemed clouded and dull as he looked back up into her face.

"I'm sorry, baby." He urged her to her feet and pulled off her gardening gloves, dropping them neatly on the ground to be dealt with later. "I'm done for the day." He paused to bring her hands to his mouth and kiss them, one at a time. "I can be here for you." He led her into the house, attempting to distract her by laying out his plans to draw her a hot bath and see to it that she had nothing to worry about for the rest of the afternoon.

The bath, wonderfully hot and perfected with a lavender, chamomile, and ylang-ylang bath bomb, had gone a long way in easing Marisol's anxiety after her eerie encounter. Later, a cuddly story time with Jude on the couch, as James made dinner in her stead, had soothed her frayed nerves completely. Now, a satisfied smile played upon her lips as she carefully turned in James's arms to face him. "Good night," she purred. She kissed his cheek, and his lips twitched up in a sleepy smile.

"Love you," he mumbled as he rolled onto his back and easily drifted off. Marisol hummed in amusement as she slipped out of bed. On her way to the bathroom, she retrieved her nightie from where it'd landed when James stripped it off her and tossed it carelessly over the side of the bed.

It was as if she could both hear and feel something snap in her brain, and Marisol suddenly threw her eyes open. Reality itself seemed to have shifted slightly off from its fixed point, leaving a tangible viciousness that she felt sinking down deep into her marrow. Instinctively, she braced herself, even clenching her jaw in inexplicable terror. Her fear was justified only moments later, when she felt the air build and shape itself into a barely perceptible mass that wrapped its claws around her ankles and slowly inched itself up along her body. She was rooted to the spot, her teeth chattering uncontrollably and her skin growing clammy as mounting dread froze the breath in her lungs. Wide-eyed and frantic, she stared at nothing as the weighted air blanketed her, pressing her deep into the mattress. She felt cool puffs of odorless, impossible breath against her neck, then along her jaw, and finally, against her ear.

"Pssst, psssst."

The hissing was soft, yet somehow so overwhelming that it drowned out even the sharp thunder of her pulse slamming against her eardrums.

"Pssst, psssssst."

Finally, Marisol's breath punched itself up from her lungs, but it was in the form of a shocked gasp as the presence pressed itself firmly against her throat.

"Nagugutom ako. Gutom na gutom na."

It began to press harder against her windpipe and spread to squeeze all around her neck. There was one final low yet loud hiss as she faded into pitch-black unconsciousness.

"Kukunin ko lahat."

When Marisol next opened her eyes, the room was bright with early morning sunshine, and James was pressing a kiss to her shoulder as his hand curled around her hip. She let out a disoriented hum, even as she pressed herself back against the comforting, solid warmth of his body. Words drifted through the cellophane haze of her mind, like fragments from a mostly forgotten dream. *I'm hungry. So hungry now.* She shuddered, and James's hand paused on her outer thigh. It moved up to wrap around her protectively instead, and he hugged her to him.

"Everything okay, baby?" His gravely morning voice sent a shock of awareness through her, but she still couldn't shake the sense of unease that felt like cotton in her throat. *I'll take everything.*

She arched back against him to ground herself in the present, where she was safe, and felt a slight twinge of guilt when it elicited a low groan and a firm press and slide of his hardness against her backside. "Not now," she murmured groggily. "Just cuddle me. Please, mahal?"

"Mmmm, not a hardship. I'll do my best to be a good boy." He chuckled, tucked her hair back behind her ear, and stretched to kiss her cheek.

"It's okay, Mari. Whatever's bothering you, I'm here." He spooned her just the way she liked best, nuzzling in close so she could fall back asleep with the periodic brush of his lips between her shoulder blades and the constant, even puff of his warm breath moving against her hair.

They both woke again some hours later, when a bright-eyed and eager Jude jumped into their bed with a happy shout of "Mommy, Daddy. It's the weekend!"

Soon enough, Marisol was too caught up in the small, myriad joys of a lazy Saturday with her precious boys to care about, or even remember, strange dreams and threatening whispers.

Kukunin ko lahat. The words from over a week ago roared in her head, alongside her thundering pulse. *I'll take everything.* Her skin was flushed and clammy, her breaths hard and too close together as panic made her muscles seize. *So hungry now.*

Marisol squeezed her eyes shut and forced herself to take a deep breath as she blindly reached out and gripped the lip of the countertop. "This can't be happening," she whimpered. She blinked a few times, expelling the tears that had welled up, before setting her gaze back on the pregnancy test. She had not wanted to bother with the uncertainty of reading lines and instead grabbed digital tests. The word *pregnant* mocked her relentlessly.

She tilted her face up and glared at the frenzied woman reflected in her bathroom mirror. Her eyes narrowed, pulling her eyebrows in toward the bridge of her nose as she did some mental calculations. They had been so careful ever since her miscarriage. They might not be able to use condoms, but Marisol tracked her cycle religiously and never missed a pill. "How?" she asked herself in a plaintive tone. "What was happening around my last period?" Her eyes rounded, her jaw went slack, and her grip on the counter tightened. Her face went ashen as it struck her: Her doctor had prescribed a new migraine medication not too long before. "Did he tell me if it would interact with my birth control? Did I just forget? Did he just assume we could fall back on condoms?" She racked her brain but could come up with nothing other than a bitter *No more Topamax for me.*

Marisol watched herself in the mirror as she slowly counted to ten in her head, taking deep breaths all the while. "And now, here I am, imagining a manananggal has come after me." A hysterical laugh burst past her lips. "Aswangs don't exist," she forcefully scolded herself. "All of them are just stories Nanay used to tell you to keep you in line and explain things she didn't want to deal with." She punctuated this with a harsh nod, as if that alone could make her fully believe her own assertions. Determined for the moment, she pushed herself off the counter and grabbed all traces of what had just transpired. She took everything out to the side yard to dispose of in their city-provided trash bin. "He can't know yet," she told herself firmly. As if in reply, she thought she heard a concerningly familiar whisper on the wind.

"Pssst, pssst."

Marisol spun on her heel, scanning her yard with a quick, desperate gaze. Seeing nothing and no one, she walked out toward the front yard. Still, she met nothing, but an odd breeze like a heavy breath shifted the strands of hair over her ear.

"Nagugutom ako."

Before she could so much as squeak in alarm, Marisol felt a presence at her back, embracing her almost as James would. It wrapped around, pressing against her abdomen as she began to shudder in fear.

"So hungry now."

A scream tore itself out of her lungs but made it past her lips as a choked sob instead. She lurched forward, falling to her knees when the presence vanished just as abruptly as it had appeared. She took only a moment or two to compose herself before she roughly pushed herself up from the ground and dusted off her pants. "No," she spat, "not this time." She clutched her stomach and swayed on the spot as she thought back to the darkest time of her life, and the event that had kicked it all off.

Her mother had tried to make their apartment aswang-proof in the aftermath of her visit to the emergency room. Even though it had clearly been too late, as if manananggal were real—a possibility Marisol was more than willing to believe now, despite the talking to she'd just given herself. Her mother had filled jars with something and tried to place them all around the apartment before James had made her leave. *What was it?* Marisol asked herself. Her expression lightened for a moment as she remembered. "Rice! Uncooked rice." Marisol had plenty of craft supplies, including mason jars in various sizes. She hurried back inside, already thinking of the best places to put them without James noticing. She would've loved to be able to call her mother, but that relationship had been strained ever since the miscarriage, and in any event, calling her for this would be like calling in the fire department and police both over some burnt bacon grease. "I've got this," she declared as she breezed through her front door.

To her great satisfaction, the rest of the day proved uneventful, and James didn't seem to notice the various mason jars hidden throughout the house. If she weren't already on edge from the burden of keeping her positive pregnancy test a secret, Marisol might've called the rest of that Friday peaceful and warm. As it was, she merely considered herself blessed to have made it all the way to bedtime without further incident. When the following day unfolded in a similar fashion, she was only a hair's breadth away from believing the old folkway of uncooked rice was working. It was as she went to check that James had locked the glass sliding door and close the blinds on her way to bed that she realized it had all been a false sense of security.

Her hand paused on the pull cord that controlled the vertical blinds when she caught movement just within her periphery. Something was creeping out from behind Jude's playhouse in the far corner of the backyard. Marisol swallowed an aborted gasp and brought her face closer to the glass, squinting to focus her sight. The animal finally came fully into view, but it was still a little too far to see clearly in the night's darkness. Whatever it was, it seemed to sit and watch Marisol curiously while she let go of the cord and instead moved to the other end of the door, to turn on the porch lights. The sudden flood of light set it scurrying into the shadows again, but the scant moments during which Marisol had a clear view were more than enough to make her back stiffen like a board. At first sight, it could've been mistaken for a small dog. Of course, then one would notice the long, whip-like tail and think again. The gray, hairless ears that flopped down the sides of its face would've further confounded any casual onlooker, but not quite as much as the almost-crocodilian shape of the creature's head, or the rodent-like feet which pointed backward.

Marisol took a shuddering breath, fighting the instinct to drop to her knees and sob. With mindless, mechanical movements, she turned the light off, checked the lock a second time, and drew the blinds shut. "Sigbin," she whispered in a childlike voice. She could hear her mother's voice in the back of her mind, reminding her, *Wherever you see a sigbin, an aswang is not far behind.* It was a few minutes before Marisol realized she was still standing in the living room, fingers curled around the pull cord, muscles stiff and face wet with tears. "But they're just stories. Aren't they?" She wanted so badly to believe that, despite all the evidence stacking up against her.

James's voice traveled across the house. "Mari, are you coming to bed?"

She managed to force out "Yes, coming" in what she deemed a convincingly calm tone, and quickly dried her eyes with the collar of her nightshirt. She took one extra moment to compose herself before giving her head a brisk shake and crossing through the living room to walk down the hall to their bedroom.

Marisol sprang up in bed, taking greedy gulps of air. An overwhelming sense of danger stabbed at each neuron in her brain, commanding her body to get out of bed and head for the door before her sense of self and awareness could catch up. Rather than clearing up, her mind felt increasingly fuzzy, and the urgent messages of *DANGER* zipping through her brain made her throat constrict reflexively. She managed to put together a single coherent thought as she turned the knob in her clammy hand and stumbled out into the hall. *Keep it together and get to Jude.* Forcing herself to breathe as deeply and evenly as possible, despite the tightness in her chest, she staggered down the hall, sliding her hand along the wall to keep herself steady. When she noticed her son's door open, the pit that had formed in her stomach suddenly felt as if it could punch through the various mucous membranes and layers of muscle to drop straight through the bottom. Taking as deep a breath as her panicked nervous system would allow, she squeezed her eyes shut and steeled herself before entering the room.

When she threw her eyes open, all the air seemed to vanish from her lungs, leaving her clutching at her throat as her eyes bulged and her brain fired off more desperate messages, reminding her muscles how to breathe. It took a millisecond to take in the scene, but it felt as if time had slowed to a snail's pace, letting Marisol's mind fully absorb the horror before her.

The first detail to firmly register was the mockingly neat way the covers had been pulled back—they lay folded over, covering Jude from the mid-thigh down. Next, she realized that her son's nightshirt had been unbuttoned and carefully pulled open to expose his torso. Marisol's eyes kept moving, following the inhuman contour of what resembled a bone-white, pencil-thin tube from the spot where it had firmly attached to Jude's soft abdomen. Her gaze continued upward along that line until it snagged on two fathomless hollows that seemed to bore into her just the same as any set of eyeballs.

Marisol quickly stunted the scream that threatened to burst from her mouth and silently pleaded with herself to process the scene faster—before her heart gave out. As if sensing her struggle, the manananggal's thin, cracked lips twitched and curved into an infernal grin around its protruding proboscis. Thin as they were, its lips still stood out like streaks of fresh blood against its corpse-like pallor. Unable to keep her gaze locked on that nightmarish face, Marisol tugged her eyes down. This time, they caught on the creature's withered breasts as they sagged, swaying obscenely with every minute flutter of the manananggal's chalky, tattered, bat-like wings. When her gaze dropped farther, Marisol's stomach churned violently at the sight of the jagged, torn flesh where the monster had separated from the rest of its body to go hunting. The lurid pink of its shredded and blood-spotted intestines assaulted her eyes as the intestines swayed with the same subtle movement as its breasts. As if she'd needed the visual cue, her nostrils flared violently with the sudden, overpowering stench of rancid meat. Marisol retched involuntarily and tasted the unsettling tang of bile on the back of her tongue.

Just then, Jude squirmed and groaned. "Mommy," he pleaded in his soft, sleep-drenched voice. He frowned and wrinkled his nose, moisture glistening at the corners of his eyes. Another whimper jerked Marisol back to her senses. As she rushed toward the bed, head woefully void of ideas, the manananggal spoke, a serpentine hiss directly in the back of her mind.

Too late.

"Too late," Marisol repeated in a desolate whisper. All the same, she climbed up into the bed and molded herself to her son's side. His head turned toward her, but his eyes remained scrunched up tight.

"It hurts, Mommy." His voice was weaker now, withering the same as his little body as the manananggal continued to feast.

Her chest felt crudely carved out, nothing left but bruised walls of ravaged muscle. The tears that streamed across her face felt mechanical, emotionless. She could only wrap her arms around her son, holding him to her as if she were trying to merge him back into her womb, and whisper against the top of his head in a voice dry as the desert, "I love you." She inhaled the crisp, clean scent of his green apple shampoo and nuzzled her cheek against his, trying to hold on to what little warmth still radiated from his small body.

It was just as she thought the obscene *schluup, schluup* of the manananggal sucking out her son's liquefied innards would rupture her mind that Marisol blinked her eyes open. She came to flat on her back, in her own bed, with James right beside her. She was already one too-tight, too-short breath away from hyperventilating, the sheets were soaked in her sweat, and her tears had plastered her hair to her skin. An agonized howl brewed low in her diaphragm, and when she sat up and turned to wake James for comfort, it erupted out of her mouth.

It took a long time being held against James's solid body and rocked gently right there, in the middle of their bed, before Marisol stopped crying, until she could fully see for herself and believe that she hadn't just woken up next to remnants of the manananggal's meal—her husband's mangled, gutless corpse. He had long since brushed her hair back and tucked it behind her ears, but a few stubborn strands remained glued to her face with sweat and tears. She shivered in his arms, disgusted by the way her nightie stuck to her clammy skin and how the wet saltiness at the corners of her mouth mingled with the off-putting taste of snot as the viscous fluid leaked freely from her nostrils.

"Tissues," she gasped, "please."

James pressed a kiss to the top of her head before getting out of bed to grab what she needed.

She gingerly plucked the box of tissues out of his hand and wiped her upper lip. She grabbed a fresh tissue and blew her nose. While he waited, James turned on the bedside lamp. Once she felt a little more human again, Marisol shifted to face him head on. Before he could ask her what terrible thing she'd dreamed of, the words "I'm pregnant" jumped past her lips.

His jaw dropped while his eyes rounded, shock overtaking his features for only a second before he collected himself. He remained silent as she wearily studied his face. She could see it clearly—in the way his shoulders had lifted, his eyes had brightened, and he had rolled his lips inward, to keep himself quiet—he was happy. He was thrilled, but he was waiting. She could read him so easily. He felt as if he needed her permission to be excited. That stung and warmed her heart in equal measure, and she felt compelled to give him her complete honesty.

"I'm scared." She hung her head. "I'm so scared, James. What if we lose it again?" She sucked in a big breath, trying to keep herself from breaking back into tears. She could feel his weight shifting, couldn't stop herself from smiling as he wrapped her up in his arms again, guiding her to rest her face in the crook of his neck. "I'm almost too scared to be pregnant," she mumbled into his skin, taking comfort and courage in how her lips moved against it. "To stay pregnant, I mean."

To his credit, he didn't falter when she made her confession; he kept up the barely perceptible swaying motion that she'd always found most soothing. "That's the fear talking," he murmured against her hair. "It's giving you ideas that don't even make sense. It's okay to be scared, Marisol." He hugged her tighter as she let out a whimper. She brought her arms up around him and squeezed, digging her nails into his back as if she were testing reality, making sure he was real. He didn't make a sound at the sudden bite of it, only kissed her again. "It's okay to be so scared that nothing makes sense." He began rubbing her back in slow circles.

After a while, he spoke again. "I can't predict the future. Nobody is going to be able to say for sure that the baby will be fine." He gently nudged her off him so that he could cup her face in his hands and look her in the eyes. She watched him, overflowing with a heartbreaking sadness, desperate for some kind of lifeline. "I'm here, though. You won't have to go through anything alone."

She attempted a smile. It was weak and fleeting, but she meant it and he seemed to know that as he smiled back. "You promise, mahal?"

"Now that's a promise I can definitely make." He leaned in and gave her a reassuring kiss. "I swear it, Mari. Whatever comes, we'll handle it together."

She nodded solemnly and grabbed another tissue. "I want my baby," she stated before blowing her nose.

James left and returned minutes later, cradling their son lovingly in his arms. Jude cracked his eyes open and let out a groggy "Daddy?" as James tried to put him back down in their bed, but they were all soon settled and falling back to sleep.

SIX MONTHS LATER

Marisol was reaching the end of her morning walk just as her new neighbor slung her purse straps over her shoulder and locked up her car. She smiled broadly when they locked eyes and then hurried over. Even before she managed to get out a greeting, her hands were reaching for Marisol's full, round belly. She caught herself and pulled back sheepishly when Marisol flinched away. "I'm so sorry," she blurted with a frantic wave of her hands. "Really, I didn't mean to be rude. It's Marisol, right?"

Marisol opened her mouth to reply, but her neighbor barreled on eagerly.

"We've never properly introduced ourselves, have we? I'm Gail." She blushed and shook her head at herself. "I don't mean to be gross, just touching your belly." There was a giddy sheen to her eyes when she glanced back into Marisol's face. "I'm just really excited, I guess." She bounced on the balls of her feet. "I'm pregnant!"

All at once, Marisol softened. She took a moment to really take in Gail's happiness. Her hazel eyes sparkled with specks of bright, cheery green and her cinnamon hair, tied back in a simple ponytail, swayed back and forth with every one of her movements. The joy seemed to radiate from her. Marisol could remember that feeling all too well. "That's wonderful! Congratulations!" She grinned at Gail with a sudden fondness. "It's okay, you can feel. Maybe she'll kick."

Gail squealed excitedly and gratefully let Marisol place her hands in the optimal spot. She continued to chat as she kept her eyes fixed on Marisol's belly. "You're having a girl? That's so exciting! Do you have a name picked out?"

Marisol's gaze flickered over to her front door, and she couldn't help but smile. "Violet."

"Beautiful." Gail glanced up only briefly. "I just can't believe this'll be me soon," she said to Marisol's belly. "I've always wanted to be a mother. I can't wait to tell my husband!" Both women gave a little cheer as they felt Violet kick out against Gail's hand, and they met each other's eyes again, beaming.

"Hindi kita iiwan," Gail said in a slow, syrupy tone.

Marisol was unsure what was more shocking: Hearing Tagalog come out of someone as fair skinned, freckled, and clearly not Filipina as Gail, or the fact that it came out in a voice not quite Gail's own.

"I'm—I'm sorry, what?"

Gail held Marisol's gaze coldly as she answered in that chilling, not-right voice, "I'll never leave you."

Marisol stumbled back, instinctively shielding her bump. She clamped her teeth down on her lower lip to keep herself from shouting out or showing too much emotion.

Gail blinked and tilted her face upward, watching her with what Marisol would've sworn was surprise and growing bewilderment, as if she'd never said a word.

"Sorry," Marisol forced herself to say as she continued backing up. "I'm suddenly feeling very tired."

"Oh." Gail frowned as she awkwardly straightened up and fidgeted with her purse straps. "I'm sorry. Umm . . . I'll let you get some rest."

Marisol didn't give Gail the opportunity to so much as raise her hand and wave before she turned and waddled the rest of the way up her front path. It wasn't until she had her fingers curled around the brass doorknob that she glanced back over her shoulder to see if her neighbor was still there.

Gail grinned, the corners of her mouth stretching wider and wider until they seemed to reach her ears, and Marisol could see far too many pearly, sharp teeth.

ABOUT THE AUTHOR

An Oregonian raised in Southern California, Lennox Rex has always been enamored with storytelling. His style has been most shaped by his earliest influences—folklore and anthology shows *The Twilight Zone* and *Are You Afraid of the Dark?*—and the work of Jack Kerouac and Patricia Highsmith. His work appears in various magazines and anthologies. *I'll Never Leave You* is his first collection. To him, life is best enjoyed with music, body mods, and plenty of coffee and sweets. He's a neurodivergent trans man living in the southern United States with his husband, their three children, a western hognose snake named Mephie, and a dog named Perona.

ACKNOWLEDGMENTS

Typing up these Acknowledgements proved to be a lot tougher than anticipated. There are so many people that, in one way or another, helped me along my journey. So many that it's impossible to name them all here, as much as I'd like to. Here's my spot to acknowledge the ones without whom I truly would not have made it here.

The first thanks go out to Sirius and the team at The Laughing Man House Publishing— for taking a chance on me and my work and giving me this platform. I'm also grateful to Mitch Green for the gorgeous art gracing my cover, to Anna at Corbeaux Editorial Services for helping me refine and polish my work, and to Holly Sivils for my epic author photo.

A handful of the stories you just read previously appeared elsewhere, in earlier forms. I'd like to thank the editors of these publications for having given my stories their first homes:

KNOW THYSELF first appeared in *Doors of Darkness: 27 Tales of Terror* in 2023.

BIRTHDAY SUIT first appeared in *Trans Rites: An Anthology of Genderfucked Horror* in 2023.

THE WITCH first appeared in the Spring 2024 issue of *Monstrous Femme Magazine*.

APPOINTED GAURDIAN first appeared in *Doors of Darkness II: Trick or Treat* in 2024.

SOME PRAYERS SHOULD GO UNANSWERED first appeared in the January 2025 issue of *Smitten Land Literary Magazine*.

ESTRANGED first appeared in the Winter 2025 issue of *A Bite of Pride eZine*.

To Leilani and Michael: Sis, thank you for being the best sibling known to existence. Michael, thank you for becoming a part of my family. I'm glad you two found each other as early on as you did— you two provided me with the healthy relationship role model that I otherwise would never have had growing up.

I can't properly express my gratitude to my husband, who's always believed in me. Honey, thank you for always alpha reading my stories no matter what happens in them. Of course, I'm not about to thank my husband without also mentioning our children. It's always going to be humbling to know those three think whatever I touch *must* be gold simply because I'm the one that made it. Just knowing the four of you exist fills me with thankfulness.

I've had many amazing teachers throughout my school years, but there are two for whom I want to make an extra effort by naming them here. Diane Ainsworth and Wendy Teasdale: I will never stop marveling at the profound impact you two have had on me. I'm so proud to know you are witnessing my success.

Beth, Carmen, and Rhiannon: Thank you all for being my first best friends. You all entered my life at such pivotal moments and supported me in so many ways. An extra little shout out to Wendy: thank you for realizing I was a bit too weird for you and instead introducing me to your twin when we were kids. You hand delivered me to my oldest friend in the world.

Ryn, Quinn, Sunny, Deb, Scholar, and Suz: Thank you all for being part of my renaissance as a writer. Your support and friendship got me through some tough times. Also, don't forget how proud I am of each one of you—you all know the different reasons why.

Daemon, Fox, Louis, and Sage: I'm so grateful for the different impacts you all have had on my burgeoning career. Thank you all for your endless support.

To you, my reader: Thank you so much for picking up a copy of I'll Never Leave You. I hope you enjoyed it. Even if you didn't, I appreciate the time you took to read my stories. This is the culmination of a lifelong dream, and it never would have happened without readers like you giving my work a shot. Thanks again, and happy reading!

CONTENT WARNINGS

Know Thyself... animal death.
The Witch... suicidal ideation.
Appointed Guardian... homophobia and transphobia.
Deathwish... suicidal ideation.
Hostile Takeover... could be triggering for survivors of physical and sexual assault due to the POV.
Some Prayers Should Go Unanswered... transphobia, childbirth, abortion, and stillbirth.
Birthday Suit... cannibalism and body horror.
I'll Never Leave You... past/off-page pregnancy loss, nightmare sequence depicting child death.